SALTWATER SUNRISES

MAGNOLIA KEY
BOOK ONE

KAY CORRELL

ZURA LU PUBLISHING LLC

Published by Zura Lu Publishing LLC

ABOUT THIS BOOK

Maxine returns to her childhood home on the charming island of Magnolia Key. She's hiding a secret and seeking refuge. Maxine reunites with her childhood friend Beverly, the owner of the beloved Coastal Coffee shop.

As Maxine navigates the complexities of rekindling old friendships and confronting her past, she finds unexpected companionship in Dale, a local with a passion for town history and owner of the quaint shop, Second Finds. Together, they explore the mysteries of a hidden painting and a mysterious, coded letter hinting at long-buried town secrets.

But as Maxine begins to find her footing, embracing the sense of belonging that Magnolia Key offers, her daughter arrives with a surprise and a request Maxine finds hard to refuse. Her past and present collide and she has impossible choices to make.

Enjoy book one in the heartwarming Magnolia Key series. Perfect for readers who love stories with a touch of romance, the charm of small-town life, and the enduring bonds of lifelong friendship.

This book is dedicated to the view out my office window. The flowing water, the wind spinner circling in the breeze, and the birds at the water's edge. And I can't forget the occasional dolphin or manatee. Such a peaceful view and the perfect place to write my stories.

KAY'S BOOKS

Find more information on all my books at
kaycorrell.com
Buy direct from Kay's Shop at
shop.kaycorrell.com

COMFORT CROSSING ~ THE SERIES

The Wedding in the Grove - (a crossover short story between series - with Josephine and Paul from The Letter.)

LIGHTHOUSE POINT ~ THE SERIES
Wish Upon a Shell - Book One
Wedding on the Beach - Book Two
Love at the Lighthouse - Book Three
Cottage near the Point - Book Four
Return to the Island - Book Five
Bungalow by the Bay - Book Six
Christmas Comes to Lighthouse Point - Book Seven

CHARMING INN ~ Return to Lighthouse Point
One Simple Wish - Book One
Two of a Kind - Book Two
Three Little Things - Book Three
Four Short Weeks - Book Four
Five Years or So - Book Five
Six Hours Away - Book Six
Charming Christmas - Book Seven

SWEET RIVER ~ THE SERIES
A Dream to Believe in - Book One
A Memory to Cherish - Book Two

A Song to Remember - Book Three
A Time to Forgive - Book Four
A Summer of Secrets - Book Five
A Moment in the Moonlight - Book Six

MOONBEAM BAY ~ THE SERIES
The Parker Women - Book One
The Parker Cafe - Book Two
A Heather Parker Original - Book Three
The Parker Family Secret - Book Four
Grace Parker's Peach Pie - Book Five
The Perks of Being a Parker - Book Six

BLUE HERON COTTAGES ~ THE SERIES
Memories of the Beach - Book One
Walks along the Shore - Book Two
Bookshop near the Coast - Book Three
Restaurant on the Wharf - Book Four
Lilacs by the Sea - Book Five
Flower Shop on Magnolia - Book Six
Christmas by the Bay - Book Seven
Sea Glass from the Past - Book Eight

MAGNOLIA KEY ~ THE SERIES
Saltwater Sunrise - Book One
Encore Echoes - Book Two

And more to come!

**WIND CHIME BEACH ~ A stand-alone
novel**

INDIGO BAY ~
Sweet Days by the Bay - Kay's Complete
Collection of stories in the Indigo Bay series

Sign up for my newsletter at my website
kaycorrell.com to make sure you don't miss any
new releases or sales.

CHAPTER 1

Beverly leaned over, annoyed that her new shoes hurt and certain they were going to cause blisters. Why had she decided that a full working day at Coastal Coffee would be a good time to wear new shoes? They were practical ones, of course. Her days of heels were long past.

She adjusted the left shoe as she poised on one foot, a bit dismayed that doing so was no longer an easy feat. Getting older wasn't for sissies. With a wobble, she lost her balance, crashed against the built-in bookcase in her office, and knocked a stack of papers to the floor. Even more annoyed at her shoes now, she leaned over to collect the pages, pausing as she noticed the bottom shelf had come loose. She jiggled the shelf, hoping to push it back in place, but it was firmly wedged in there crooked now. The shoes, the mess of papers, and now the shelf? Her usual look-on-the-bright-side outlook was failing her.

With a sigh, she knelt down to fix the shelf, surprised when it slipped out easily in her hands. There, underneath the shelf, was a hidden compartment. How could she not have known about this after owning Coastal Coffee for all these years? She reached inside and pulled out a rolled-up canvas.

What could be important enough to hide in a secret compartment? Curiosity pricked the back of her neck. She got up and moved over by the window, carefully unrolling the canvas. She frowned as she peered at it. It looked slightly like Magnolia Key, yet different enough that she knew it wasn't. But the building in it looked very similar to the one that used to be at the ferry landing. Though a storm had taken out that building years ago.

She frowned. Why had it been hidden away in the bookcase? She scanned it, looking to see if the artist had signed it, but found no signature. The painting depicted old-time fishing boats, with the sunrise just beginning to illuminate the bay. But the sunrise came at the landing in this painting from a different angle than the sun hit the landing here on the island. Was this a real place or just something from an artist's imagination?

A loud crash sounded from out in the cafe, and Beverly whirled around. Now what? She hurriedly set the painting on her desk and rushed to see what had happened.

A mess of broken dishes and spilled food lay splattered across the floor beside a table of four customers. She stifled a sigh and struggled to put on a smile, pretending everything was just fine even though the new server had dropped a tray of dishes. Again. The girl was friendly and kind but had a habit of letting dishes shatter all around her.

Beverly hurried over, grabbing a tub to help pick up the broken pieces.

"I'm so sorry. I'm so clumsy. I'll pay for them." Janine was almost in tears.

"That's okay. It happens." She quickly picked up the pieces, assured the customers she would rush their order through again, and headed to the kitchen.

As she pushed into the kitchen, the enticing

3

aroma of freshly ground coffee beans along with the cinnamony goodness of sweet bread warming in the oven assaulted her senses. She dumped the broken dishes and ruined food in the trash and headed over to the cook. "We need that last order remade."

Sal raised his eyebrows. "She dropped one again?"

"She's new. She's learning." In Janine's defense, she had picked up on the menu, the routine, memorized the specials each day. She just hadn't quite figured out how to not drop trays of food.

"I'll hurry and remake it."

She nodded and headed back out into the cafe. The morning sped by and the breakfast crowd emptied out, chasing all thoughts of the painting from her mind. She chatted with customers, cleared tables, and glanced at the clock. The breakfast rush merged into the lunch crowd.

Things sure had changed since she'd opened Coastal Coffee over thirty years ago. At that time, the shop was one-third this size. She'd served coffee and a few different breakfast pastries from six a.m. until one p.m. She'd been the only worker and worked six days a week.

But as the business grew, she expanded into the shop next door and extended her hours. She served sandwiches and soups for lunch now, too, and closed around three p.m. Thankfully, the business growth had allowed her to hire more workers. These days she vowed to only work five days a week but rarely kept that promise. Something always seemed to need her attention and lure her back to the shop.

Before she knew it, the lunch crowd had come and then thinned out. She glanced at the clock again. How did time seem to go by in a flash and yet seem to crawl at the same time?

She knew it was just the anticipation of seeing her friend Maxine again. Anticipation and a bit of apprehension. She hadn't seen Maxine in over ten years. And during the two decades before that, Maxine had only made a handful of trips back here to Magnolia Key.

It had been so hard at first when Maxine married and left the island. They'd grown up together, inseparable from day one. Their mothers had been best friends, and it was inevitable that she and Maxine became best friends, too. There had never been a secret between them. At least not back then.

She still considered Maxine her best friend,

even if they only spoke half a dozen times a year now. Probably less than that in recent years, honestly. She wondered what Maxine thought about her now. She'd never left the island, never wanted to. Except for that one brief time when she actually thought she would sell Coastal Coffee and leave. But that hadn't worked out at all.

Anyway, Maxine had married Victor, who rapidly climbed the corporate ladder. Bought a fancy big house—she'd seen photos of it—and they had two beautiful kids. A perfect life. And so different from hers.

It was strange to think about how their paths had split and they'd ended up in such dissimilar places.

She pushed the thoughts away and hauled another tray of dishes back to the kitchen. After rinsing them, she placed them in the dishwasher. Drying her hands with a nearby towel, she ran her gaze around the kitchen. Everything in place. That was one of her rules. Everything back in place before closing for the day.

Sal was busy getting things set up for the next day. She recently switched to getting the breakfast pastries and desserts from Julie's Sweet Shoppe over on Belle Island, and they were a big hit. It freed up the time that would otherwise be spent baking. They were busy enough with other tasks at the shop. And, honestly, Julie was a much more accomplished baker than either she or Sal would ever be.

She popped back out into the shop and glanced at the old antique clock hanging on the wall over the coffee bar. Maxine had said she'd be here this afternoon, but no sign of her yet. Every time Maxine returned for a visit, Beverly wondered if it would still be the same. The last visit, over ten years ago, had been strained, and she feared their bonds of friendship were dying. But her grandmother always said that true friendship survives everything. Time. Distance. Troubles. She just hoped her grandmother was right.

Maxine stood on the upper deck of the ferry as it plunged through the waters of the bay, heading for Magnolia Key. Her car was safely stowed below, filled with her belongings. Enough for a good long stay back here in Magnolia. She hadn't mentioned that to Beverly. Hadn't mentioned that this visit was more than her usual two- or three-day stay. But then, there were a lot of things she hadn't been able to make herself explain to Beverly when they chatted. And those phone calls were few and far between the last few years. Totally her fault. She'd just been so busy.

And lost.

And struggling.

She glanced over to the right and saw the huge expanse of a bridge being built to connect the island with the mainland. That would be a big change after all the years of needing a boat or the ferry to get over to the island. But change was inevitable. She knew that better than most.

She stood there drinking in the view, feeling the salty breeze toss her curls this way and that, and not caring one bit what she looked like. The air was cleansing, her tension melted away as she got closer to the island.

When the ferry chugged up to the landing, she went below and slipped into her car. She waited her turn while the other cars filed off the ferry. And then, there she was, back on the island.

She turned down Landing Street, appropriately named years ago for its ferry landing, and then turned down Main Street, heading toward Coastal Coffee. She parked across the street from it as the anxiety that she thought had been swept away in the sea breeze crept back through her. She had so much to tell Beverly. So much she *had* to tell her. It wasn't possible to keep it a secret any longer.

But maybe she shouldn't have returned. Maybe this was a big mistake. Maybe she should have tried yet again in Philadelphia to make a go of it. But how many failures could she handle?

Then when she finally lost the house and needed to move, Magnolia Key called to her. Beckoned her home. Although she never thought she'd be coming back here under these circumstances.

But was it really home anymore? Her parents had died when her kids were young. She had no siblings. No family back here. And her grown kids? Not likely that they'd be coming here anytime soon. She hadn't even been back in more than ten years. Hadn't lived here in more than thirty.

And yet... she so wanted it to feel like home to her again. Wanted to feel like she belonged here. Belonged anywhere.

She glanced in the rearview mirror and for a

brief moment half-expected the younger version of herself to be looking back at her. The one without any gray hair and without wrinkles stubbornly clinging to the corners of her eyes. She dragged her fingers through her hair, trying to tame the curls into some semblance of a hairstyle. Lines of stress were etched clearly in her features.

What would Beverly think of her now?

She climbed out of the car and stood for a moment, looking at the weathered wooden sign across the street. Coastal Coffee.

A hint of jealousy crept through her at everything Beverly had done with her life. The successful business she ran. Maxine shook her head, chasing away thoughts of her own failures. She resolutely crossed the street and took a deep breath before opening the door.

The familiar sights and sounds and aroma of the shop wrapped around her. The worn wooden floorboards—slightly uneven—and the cheerful light spilling in through the large windows. The big chalkboard that hung over the coffee bar proclaiming the day's specials in Beverly's flowing handwriting.

Her nervousness mounted until her eyes met Beverly's from across the room. Beverly's smile was genuine and welcoming as she held out her arms. She rushed across the distance and threw herself into her friend's embrace. The years melted away as they stood there wrapped in each other's arms.

"It's good to have you back," Beverly said as she finally pulled back.

Maxine did her best to keep her tears from spilling over. She swallowed. "It's good to be back." She stepped back awkwardly.

"I was just getting ready to put up the closed sign. But come, I'll get us some coffee. Do you want to sit?"

"I don't know. I've been in the car for hours."

"Okay, I'll get us some to-go cups. We can walk along the boardwalk."

"Sounds great."

Within minutes, they were heading out into the sunshine and onto the boardwalk that stretched for a mile or so along the shoreline. Memories of walking along it when they were younger flooded her mind. Getting snow cones from the vendor who sold them during the summer season. Grabbing ice cream cones and wandering down the walkway, chatting about schoolwork, boys, their teachers. A wave of nostalgia swept over her.

"So, how long can you stay this time?" Beverly interrupted her thoughts.

"I..." She wasn't ready to discuss it all. Not yet. "I'm not sure. Awhile."

Beverly looked at her closely. "You don't have to get back to Victor and the kids?"

Now was probably the time to tell her the truth, but she chickened out. "I... no, I don't have to get back anytime soon. I just need a little... vacation."

"Great. Magnolia is the perfect place for that."

"I booked a room at Darlene's B&B." Though she couldn't stay there long. She didn't want to blow through the little money she did have.

"You could have stayed with me."

"In your one bedroom over the shop?"

"Oh, didn't I tell you? I finally moved out of there. Bought a cute little place on the beach. It was a fixer-upper, so I got it for a great price. Did the work bit by bit the last few years. Finally moved in a couple of months ago. Now the space above the shop is storage."

"I didn't know." So many things they didn't know about each other anymore.

"If you change your mind or get tired of the B&B, my door is always open."

"Thanks." At least she'd have a place to stay after she left the B&B. At least for a little while. She didn't want to wear out her welcome. And she needed to find a job ASAP. Hopefully, one that she could succeed at this time and not get fired from like her last two jobs.

She had to admit, the first time she got fired she probably deserved it. It was so hard to adjust to going back to work full time after staying home and raising the kids and taking care of Victor's whims for so many years. But she had to get a job. Bring in money. Support herself.

And she'd been silly to try to hang onto the house. She couldn't afford the payments. Not on any job she'd been able to find. A degree in education didn't mean much if you hadn't used it in thirty years. Now that the house was sold— and she'd really had no choice—she had a small sum of money left from the sale. And her car. And that was about it. She'd sold most of the furniture and banked that money too.

She was ready for a new beginning.

Wasn't she?

~

Darlene greeted Maxine as she entered the B&B. "Maxine, it's so great to see you. How many years has it been?"

"About ten since I've been back."

"Well, we're glad to have you. I gave you the upper suite."

"Oh, just a regular room is fine." And all she could afford.

"Nonsense. The upgrade is on me. It's just up the stairs and to the left. Last room. It's a corner room with a great view."

"Thank you. That's so nice of you." She took the key and went upstairs. She opened the door and sunlight spilled around her from the bank of windows on both corner walls. A large queen-sized bed sat against another wall, placed so that you could see the view from it. A fluffy white chenille bedspread covered the bed. An overstuffed chair and small table were placed beside the windows. A braided rug covered the worn floorboards. The inviting, welcoming atmosphere of the room surrounded her.

How could a room in a B&B make her feel more at home than the big old house she'd shared with Victor? Pride had made her struggle to keep that house, but once it was gone, she had to admit she felt a sense of relief. It was a house, not a home. Victor had chosen it and surprised her. She had no say in it. But then, a lot of their marriage had been like that.

She shoved all thoughts of Victor far, far away and set her suitcase on a wooden rack. She carefully hung her clothes in the closet and took her toiletries to the bathroom. It was large and painted a pale mint color, with thick, thirsty white towels hung on the racks.

This was so nice. Nicer than the apartment she'd had after selling the house. That apartment had been a dump. Worn carpeting. Frayed curtains in the two small windows. Walls as thin as paper. A shower that only had hot water on occasion so that she'd almost adjusted to freezing showers. A small kitchenette. It had been in a questionable part of town but had been all she could afford.

She'd finally decided enough was enough. Now she had most of her things stashed in the trunk of her car. They'd be fine there for now. She had one small storage unit back home that she needed to get rid of soon so she could quit paying rent on it. But she kept hoping she'd find a place to live and could arrange to bring her things here.

If she decided to stay here in Magnolia Key.

And that was a big if at this point. But really, where else did she have to go?

CHAPTER 2

Beverly walked through the shop, unlocked the front door to Coastal Coffee, and flipped the sign to open. She'd already been here for an hour after picking up the pastry order from the first ferry. Julie sent it over every morning.

She wondered how things would change with the new bridge going in. It most likely would be good for business. Though she was a little worried it would change the small-town feeling on Magnolia Key. They'd probably get more day tourists. People just wanting a quick break at the beach. There was talk of changing some zoning laws to allow taller buildings on the island. She wasn't a fan of that. She wasn't against progress, per se, but part of the appeal of Magnolia was its quaintness. They had some visitors who came back year after year, generation after generation. Would they still come if the island became more commercial?

The door opened, and Nash Carlisle stepped inside. "Morning, Beverly."

"Morning, Nash." Nash was her first customer Monday through Friday before he headed out to work at his construction job. The company that had been owned by his daddy before Nash took it over.

"Morning, Beverly."

"I've got some of those strawberry muffins from Julie today."

"Perfect. I'll take one of those with my coffee." He headed over to his table after stopping to pick up one of the copies of the newspaper she always had waiting for her customers—the papers also came over on the first early morning ferry. A lot of people got their news online now, but she still liked to provide her customers with a copy of the paper to peruse with their coffee if they preferred it.

More customers came in and she fell into her familiar routine. Getting them pastries and coffee. Chatting about this and that. And the weather. People were always commenting on the weather.

"Going to get some showers this afternoon."

"Mighty fine breeze this morning."

"Heard the temps are going to hit record highs next week."

"My bones say some rain is heading this way."

And so her day began. Soon Eleanor Griffin came in as she always did on Tuesday and Friday mornings, settling into the same table in the corner she always sat in—unless some unfortunate soul didn't know it was Eleanor's table. Then she would take the table beside it and read the paper with much sighing and rustling of the pages and occasional dagger-throwing glances at the unlucky patrons. As soon as they would leave, Eleanor would move to her table and order her breakfast. Beverly had considered placing a reserved sign on the table on Tuesdays and Fridays, but really everyone in the town knew Eleanor sat there. Though, when the bridge did finally open, she supposed a reserved sign was probably the practical solution.

Beverly headed over with a pot of coffee, a pitcher of fresh cream, and a coffee cup. "Morning, Miss Eleanor." Everyone in town called her Miss Eleanor.

"Good morning, Beverly. I see you have some of those chocolate-filled scones," she said, glancing at the chalkboard above the coffee bar. "I believe I'll have one of those with my coffee."

"Sure thing. Be back in a sec." She returned with the scone, slightly heated just like Eleanor liked her pastries, and set it on the table.

Eleanor nodded and went back to her paper. Not quite dismissing Beverly, but almost. But everyone knew Eleanor liked her privacy. Kept to herself with her daily routine. Her twice weekly trips to Coastal Coffee. A trip to the market every Monday morning at ten. She walked her dog—an aging Cavalier King Charles named Winston—every morning at seven and afternoon at four. She never missed a Sunday at church and sat in the second row of pews in the seats the Whitmores had sat in for generations. Miss Eleanor had been born a Whitmore, then married Theodore Griffin. But most of the town still considered her a Whitmore, a family that had been on the island since the first settlers.

Beverly realized she was still standing beside the table when Eleanor looked up questioningly.

"Oh, sorry. Lost in thought for a moment."

Eleanor bobbed her head. "I'm sure you have other customers to wait on."

"Yes, ma'am." Beverly didn't know why the comment made her feel like a scolded schoolgirl.

A half hour later, Eleanor folded her paper. That was Beverly's clue to give Eleanor her check. She hurried over with it and set it on the table.

"Beverly, I didn't see your name on the list of donors to the fundraiser for the town park." Eleanor cocked her head slightly to one side, pinning Beverly with a look that would not let go.

"I… um… I just haven't gotten around to it yet. I will. Soon. I promise." She'd have to come up with a donation quickly now.

"I expect to hear from you soon." Eleanor bobbed her head slightly as if there was never a question that Beverly would do as she was told.

Maxine entered Coastal Coffee much later than she'd planned to. She hadn't realized how exhausted she was from the stress. She'd woken up with light streaming in the windows and missed the whole breakfast part of the B&B. She'd hurriedly gotten dressed and walked over to Beverly's shop.

As soon as she entered, the relaxed beauty of the coastal decor greeted her. Faded shades of teal, mint, and coral melded perfectly with the wooden chairs and tables that were polished to a shine. Warm sunlight streamed in through the front windows and danced across the worn floorboards. The unmistakable aroma of freshly ground coffee mixed with the tantalizing smells of the fresh baked goods warming in the oven. The low murmur of the customers swirled around her.

Coastal Coffee was welcoming in the same way Magnolia Key was as a whole—they both opened their arms to locals and visitors alike. A tangible sense of warmth and community surrounded her. She stood for a moment, drinking in the sights and sounds until the door opened behind her and the gentle sound of the wind chimes outside drifted in along with an older couple. They looked familiar, but she couldn't quite remember their names.

The woman smiled. "Ah, Maxine, I heard you were back in town. So good to see you."

Was this gray-haired lady with the cane really Judy McNally? Last she'd seen Judy, she'd been a forty-something, fit blonde who ran the beach daily. "Judy, Harv, so great to see you, too," she said, pleased that she'd recognized them.

"Been a long time," Harv said as he took Judy's elbow. "Bet Beverly is thrilled you could visit."

She thought there was a bit of reproach in his voice. Or maybe it was her own guilt poking her for staying away for so long. He led Judy to a table against the far wall.

Maxine spied Beverly in the corner talking to Miss Eleanor, of all people. Great. If she'd just been a bit later, maybe she could have avoided Eleanor altogether. She pasted on what she hoped was a genuine-looking smile and headed over to the corner.

"Miss Eleanor. How great to see you." Did that sound genuine?

Eleanor looked her over from top to bottom, sizing her up before she spoke. "Ah, Maxine. You're back for a visit. How long has it been? A long time, I believe." Eleanor's brow creased in disapproval, like she couldn't believe anyone would stay away from Magnolia that long.

"It's been—" She caught herself right before admitting it had been ten years. "It's been a while."

"So, why are you back?" Eleanor eyed her suspiciously as if she didn't belong here.

"Um… for a visit?" That wasn't the whole truth, but enough for Eleanor to know.

"I see. Well, if you're still here next week, we need more volunteers for the fundraiser for the town park. You should sign up." Eleanor stood, placed some bills on the table, and turned to leave.

"Nice seeing you," Maxine said, trying her best to feel like Eleanor wasn't judging her. Though really, the woman *had* been judging her. But then, that was nothing new. Eleanor judged everyone and found most people lacking. Not up to the Whitmore standings. When she and Beverly were teenagers, it used to scare her when Miss Eleanor would pin her with one of her looks. But now? It kind of just annoyed her. Pretty much so. She did admit a moment of panic when Eleanor had given her the once-over glance.

Eleanor swept out of the coffee shop, and

Maxine let out a long breath. Beverly laughed. "Miss Eleanor will never change. And don't worry. She just had me apologizing, too. She always seems to reduce me to some clueless teenager when she speaks to me." Beverly's eyes twinkled. "Come on, let's get you some breakfast. On the house."

"You don't have to do that."

"It's not often my best friend comes for a visit."

Guilt swept through her. She'd have to tell Beverly the truth. And soon. She just dreaded what her friend would think of her when she heard why she'd returned.

"Take a seat, and I'll bring us out coffee. Janine can finish up the breakfast crowd." Beverly sighed. "If she doesn't end up dropping someone's breakfast."

Maxine settled into a seat at the nearest table—but not Miss Eleanor's, even though she was gone. No use tempting fate.

Beverly returned with two muffins and coffee and sat across from her. "So, what are your plans while you're here? I took tomorrow off if you want to go to the beach. Or do you still like to go antiquing? There's that secondhand shop here in town. Second Finds.

Lots of things to browse through. And Saturday night there's a concert at the gazebo if you're still here. A barbershop quartet. They're actually pretty good."

Now was the time to speak up. Tell her. And yet, the words wouldn't come.

Beverly frowned. "You okay?"

"I am…" She paused and looked directly at Beverly. "No, I'm not."

The wrinkles in Beverly's brow deepened. "What's wrong?"

"I… I have to tell you the truth."

"You can tell me anything. You know that." Beverly reached over and took one of her hands, squeezing it. "Just… tell me."

She sucked in a deep breath. "I… Well, actually… Victor. Victor divorced me."

Beverly's eyes widened. "He did? When?"

She looked down at the table and fiddled with the spoon next to her coffee cup before looking back up. "A couple of years ago."

Beverly sat back in her chair. "A couple of years? Why didn't you tell me?"

"Because… I just felt like such a failure. I spent all those years trying to be the perfect wife, perfect mother. Then one day he just comes home, packs a suitcase, and says he's leaving. He found someone new." She closed her eyes. "And wow, is his new girlfriend a looker. She's about twenty years younger. Gorgeous. Blonde hair. I swear she's barely a size two."

"But why do you feel like a failure if the jerk cheated on you and left you?"

"It's not just that."

"Go on. Tell me." Beverly encouraged her with a nod.

"The divorce settlement didn't go well. I got the house and not much else. But then, I couldn't really afford that big house. I got a job, of course. But, then… I lost it. And then got another job and lost that one, too. Then it was hard to find another one. I ended up selling the house and moved into this tiny one-room apartment. My kids look at me like I'm this big failure. And I just… I just up and packed up my things and headed back here to Magnolia."

"Why didn't you tell me all this while you were going through it? I could have…" Beverly shrugged. "I don't know what I could have done, but I would have been there to support you."

"I just thought I could sort it out. Stand on my own two feet. Get a job. Support myself. But nothing worked out like I hoped."

"I'm glad you came back here. It's where you belong. Magnolia Key is your home."

"Is it? It doesn't really feel that way anymore."

Beverly nodded vigorously. "Yes, it is your home. And we're going to sort all this out. I promise. Sometimes you have to do some searching to find out where you belong. And I truly believe you belong here in Magnolia now."

"Maybe." She still wasn't certain of that. "But first of all, I need a job. I don't really have much savings."

"Lucky for you, I need another worker here at Coastal Coffee. Bonus if you don't repeatedly drop trays of food." Beverly grinned.

"Are you sure? You're not just saying that to help me out?"

"Nope, I need the help. And why don't you move in with me while you get your feet under you? No use spending that money at Darlene's."

"I don't want to put you out."

"Nonsense. I have a three-bedroom cottage. I have plenty of room. I'll meet you there later this afternoon and we'll get you set up. It's number seven, Seaside Avenue."

"I really appreciate all this." A tiny bit of

hope sprang up inside her. Maybe coming back here wasn't such a bad idea after all.

"Don't mention it. It's what friends are for." Beverly gave her a warm smile. One that held no judgment. And for that, she was very grateful.

CHAPTER 3

Maxine checked out of Darlene's and loaded up her car with her things. Darlene had wished her luck with her new job and seemed genuinely happy that Maxine was staying in Magnolia.

She had time until she was supposed to meet Beverly, so she drove around town a bit. The old school looked the same. A one-story building that held kindergarten through high school. Not very large since there weren't a lot of kids on the island. Back when she and Beverly were in school, they'd had two grades combined in one classroom. She wondered if they still did that. Some families had sent their kids over on the ferry to the high school on the mainland. Would things change when the bridge was finished?

Would more parents opt to send their kids to school on the mainland?

So much might change. She imagined the boardwalk would be filled with people coming over for the day to enjoy the beach. But the shops along the boardwalk would benefit from more customers. There were a few motels scattered along the beach. They would probably all be filled if it got easier to get to the island.

Right now it still looked amazingly like it had when she was a girl. A sleepy little beach town. Almost picture-postcard perfect.

She glanced at the time and drove down Seaside, looking for number seven. She pulled into the drive beside an old station wagon. Beverly was never going to give that vehicle up until she absolutely had to. It had to be twenty years old by now.

She grabbed her suitcase from the back seat and went up to the front door. Beverly opened it before she even had time to knock. "Come in, come in." Beverly reached for the suitcase. "Let me show you your room, and then we can bring in anything else you have in your car that you want in."

Beverly's cottage was bright and airy. She'd

decorated it with understated coastal decor and comfortable-looking furniture. The main room had a wall of windows offering a view of the gulf.

"This is lovely."

"Thanks. It was mostly a labor of love. It was kind of rundown when I bought it. But I loved working on it."

She followed Beverly down the hall and into a nice-sized bedroom on the front side of the house. "The bathroom's just down the hall." Beverly pointed.

"I really appreciate this. Once I get my feet under me, I promise I'll look for a place of my own."

"There's no hurry. I'll enjoy the company."

Beverly helped her bring in a few boxes of her things, then left her to get settled. She hung up her clothes and finished unpacking. Afterward she found Beverly in the kitchen, making iced tea.

"I thought we could go sit outside on the deck. I could use some time off my feet."

They headed outside with large glasses of tea, the ice tinkling in the glasses, and settled onto two Adirondack chairs facing the water. She slowly relaxed as they sat and sipped their tea. The stress of the last few months—few years—slowly started to fade away.

"So I know I said I took tomorrow off, but it looks like Janine needs the day off. Taking her mother to the doctor on the mainland."

"That's okay. I could start working tomorrow. You could show me what to do. I haven't waited tables since that summer we worked at Sharky's." She frowned. "Is Sharky's still here?"

"Still here. Still has the same menu filled with fried food." Beverly grinned. "And it's still really good."

"We should go there."

Beverly nodded. "We will."

"How early do you go into work?"

"I pick up the bakery order at six a.m., then head into the coffee shop after that. Sal is usually already there getting things going."

"Okay, I'll be up and ready to go." She swore she was not going to let Beverly down. She'd be good at this job and really help out. At least she hoped she wouldn't disappoint Beverly and get fired from this job like the last handful she'd had.

They sat outside for a long time, with Beverly filling her in on town gossip. What was going on. Who had moved to town, who had moved away.

"And I have to figure out something to donate to the fundraiser. Miss Eleanor made me promise." Beverly laughed. "I'll think of something."

"And I guess I'm volunteering for it, too. Because she's sure to hear I'm staying in town and will demand—I mean, *expect*—me to." Maxine laughed. "She's still a force to be reckoned with, isn't she?"

"She is, and I think she always will be. No matter how much she ages."

"She must be, what? Close to seventy or seventy-five now?"

"I'd imagine so, not that she'd ever tell her age."

"Any of her family still live on the island?"

"No, they've all moved away. Her one granddaughter comes to visit fairly often, though. That's about it. Haven't seen her other family in years."

"So she still lives in that big old house all alone?"

"Just Miss Eleanor and her dog, Winston."

Maxine frowned. "I wonder if she's lonely."

"Miss Eleanor was kind of a loner, even

when she was married and her kids were young." Beverly leaned back in her chair and stretched out her legs.

"Or maybe the word you were looking for was aloof."

"That, too. I'm not sure many people measure up to her expectations. I'm thinking that's why her kids all fled town as soon as they were old enough. Remember how strict she was with them?"

"Only that oldest son of hers turned out to be the wildest boy in town, didn't he?" Maxine shook her head.

Beverly's eyes widened for a moment, then she gave a rueful smile. "He was certainly always full of surprises."

Beverly got quiet and looked lost in thought. Ah, well. Memories had a way of doing that, didn't they?

CHAPTER 4

Beverly was pleased that Maxine caught on quickly to working at Coastal Coffee. By the third day, she was a pro. Handling orders, refilling coffee, and helping out in the kitchen. Quite a few of the regulars knew Maxine from when she was growing up on the island and were pleased to see her. It appeared this was going to work out for both of them.

Maxine offered to work more hours when Janine needed time off when her mother needed yet more doctor appointments. She didn't know what she would have done if Maxine hadn't popped up when she did.

As they were closing up after the lunch crowd left, Beverly paused and looked over at an empty wall near the coffee bar. "You know. I think that wall needs a bookcase on it. A small one should fit. And we could fill it with books. I've always wanted a lending library here. People could grab a book and return it or donate one that they'd finished. Might be easier than always having to go over to the mainland to the library or the bookstore."

"That's a great idea."

"I've got some accounting to do before I leave today, but how about you go over to Second Finds and see if you can pick out a bookcase that will work? You always did have a good eye for that kind of stuff, and I know you love antiquing."

"I'd love to do that. Does Ginger Bailey still run it?"

"No, her nephew, Dale, runs it now. Ginger passed away a few years ago."

"Oh, that's too bad. She was such a nice lady."

"Anyway, if you find something, Dale will send me an invoice for it. I'm always getting something from him. Replaced some chairs here at the cafe. And that picture over there..." She paused and pointed. "I got that from him too.

Not sure who painted it, but someone did years ago. It's that little cove off the bay. Remember going there?"

"I do. It's so peaceful there." Maxine glanced at the painting. "It had to have been quite a while ago. See, the old lean-to structure was still there. It was in ruins by the time we were kids."

"The painting isn't signed, and Dale—even though he's kind of a history buff when it comes to the island—didn't have any ideas."

"I don't remember a Dale from when I lived here."

"He's a few years older than us, but he used to come here in the summers to visit his aunt. He moved here right after you left town. He came to the island to help Ginger out after she took a bad fall. He ended up taking over Second Finds and staying here."

"I'll head over there after we finish closing up the shop."

Beverly went back to her office and sat down. The painting she'd found was still loosely rolled up on one edge of the desk. She should show it to Dale. Maybe he'd know more about it. Though, probably not since it wasn't of

Magnolia Key. With that decision made, she flipped open her laptop and got to work.

Maxine headed over to Second Finds after helping Beverly close up Coastal Coffee. The warm sunshine greeted her as she strolled down the sidewalk. A few people recognized her and said hi. That pleased her but still didn't make her feel like she actually belonged here. Maybe eventually she would.

She got to Second Finds and pushed into the shop. A bell jangled over the door and she smiled as it brought back memories of stopping in the shop when she was young. Ginger always let her browse around. The familiar smell of the shop surrounded her. Old books, worn leather, and the faint scent of lemon from the polish on the furniture. Ginger always made the furniture shine. She glanced around at the old furniture, vintage clothing, and various items from bygone eras that had found their way into the shop—an eclectic mix of things all long forgotten by their owners.

She walked into the shop and ran her fingers over the spine of an old book, the title almost worn off the well-loved tome. A glass doorknob caught the light of an antique chandelier, scattering rainbow flashes onto a table. A feeling of stepping into the past came over her as she wandered deeper into the shop.

Suddenly, a man appeared down the aisle. "Good afternoon. May I help you find something?" His smile was friendly, welcoming.

"You must be Dale." There was a smattering of gray at his temples, and his blue eyes peered out from reading glasses settled low on his nose. He wasn't much taller than she was. Maybe five-ten or so.

"I am." He nodded.

"I'm Maxine Shipman. Beverly sent me looking for a bookcase for Coastal Coffee. She's thinking of putting in a small lending library at the coffee shop."

"What a great idea. Here, I have some bookcases back this way." He snatched off his glasses and slipped them into his shirt pocket and led the way down the aisle.

A well-lit area in the back was filled with larger pieces of furniture, all polished and waiting for someone to want them again. Appreciate them. A tall bookcase, but not too deep, caught her attention. "This one might work. Look at the detail carved into the piece of wood going across the top. It's lovely."

"That one is kind of beat up. I try to do my best to make the pieces look good, but that one has some deep scratches. And I had to glue the side. See, right here." He pointed to the split. "It's sturdy, but needs some love."

"Oh, you know what I could do? I could paint it with chalk paint. Maybe a nice muted teal color. That would look great with Beverly's decor in the shop."

"There are initials on the back of it. JB. I assume it's the initials of the woodworker."

She peered at the back, tracing her finger over the initials, then came to the front and ran her fingers along the worn wooden shelves. "I think this will work perfectly."

"I can deliver it tomorrow. How about right about three or so after Beverly closes? I have a part-time worker who will be here tomorrow afternoon."

"That will be fine. I'm working then. I just need to find a place to work on it a bit. I'll ask Beverly. Then all I need to do is find some books to add to it." She took one last look at the bookcase, sure that Beverly would love it. "I guess I'll see you tomorrow, then."

"I'll see you tomorrow." He smiled at her, his eyes twinkling with warmth.

She turned to leave but couldn't help stopping to look at quite a few items as she was leaving the shop. There was one small table with an unusual shape, but the wood and finish were in bad shape. It would look adorable painted a pastel shade and used for a bed table or small table beside a couch. She had no money for things like this now, but soon, after she found a place of her own, she'd be back to shop here.

Maxine and Beverly had a light dinner that night, then went outside to watch the sunset. "You're really going to love the bookcase. Such great workmanship. And Dale made sure it was sturdy. With a bit of paint on it, I think it would brighten up that wall, too. I'm going to put a slight glaze on it to make the carving near the top of the bookcase really pop."

"I defer to your guidance. I know you have an eye for that kind of thing. You could paint it in the storage room in the back of the shop. There's a window in there, so you should get some nice light."

"That would be perfect. It will take a few coats and sanding in between. Then I'll put a protective finish on it." She paused, wondering if wax or a polyurethane finish would be better. But she loved the feel of a wax finish. She was leaning that way.

"You sound like you've done this before."

"I have. I love restoring furniture. Either sanding and restaining or painting if the pieces need it." She still had a few pieces of furniture she'd redone that were back in storage. Along with a queen bed with a headboard she'd found at a thrift shop and refinished.

"I can't wait to get the lending library started." Beverly leaned back in her chair and watched the flight of a pair of gulls swooping down by the water.

"I'm sure it will be used a lot. It's a great idea."

Beverly turned back to her. "You know, Dale's a great guy. He's really gotten into the history of Magnolia Key. He's done a lot of research. He has a small section at Second Finds dedicated to the history of the island."

"He does seem nice." And handsome. *Now, where had that thought come from?*

"Well, I think I'm going to head in and do

some reading. Or at least try to keep my eyes open long enough to read. I'm beat." Beverly got up and headed inside.

Maxine sat outside, watching the stars begin to twinkle in the sky. It was so very peaceful sitting out here. She put her feet up on a footrest and leaned back, relaxing.

She was pleased at how quickly she'd caught on to working at Coastal Coffee. She didn't want to let Beverly down. The extra hours she picked up were nice, too. Beverly paid a fair wage, and the tips were decent. She wanted to add to her savings and find a place of her own. So maybe, finally, she'd feel like she wasn't depending on someone else.

She'd been more than happy to look for the bookshelf to help Beverly out. She loved going to antique shops and secondhand stores looking for furniture and other items. Not that she'd had the money to do that recently. But when she and Victor were first married and didn't have much money, she furnished their house with old antique finds she'd discovered. Once Victor rose up the company ladder and his earnings skyrocketed, he'd demanded the old furniture go. He'd hired an interior designer to decorate the huge house he got them. In the right area of town, of course. The house wasn't one she would have picked out. It had no life, no spark. But it sure was big, and Victor loved that.

It had a huge dining room where she threw business dinner parties. The room was filled with an expensive dining room set that cost more than all she'd earned—combined—from the jobs she'd had the last couple of years. But Victor had taken that dining room set with him for the new—bigger—house he'd purchased when he divorced her.

But she'd naively thought they were happy there raising the kids. She was always chauffeuring the kids around to their activities. Victor would show up at an occasional sports game or school event. Enough that he could look like the concerned, involved father. Though he never wanted to be bothered by details of the kids' lives or schedules. But she'd handled all that. Made sure they were where they were supposed to be, when they were supposed to be.

But none of that mattered when Victor walked in and announced he was divorcing her. No question of marriage counseling or a trial separation. He just... moved on. Her heart clutched remembering the day he'd come home from work. She had dinner waiting in the oven for him. He never really let her know when he would be home so she'd grown used to making sure she made something she could keep warm.

But that day he came in, threw some papers on the kitchen table, and declared they were getting divorced. She'd been too shocked to cry. To even question him. He went upstairs, and she stared at the legal papers.

He came downstairs fifteen minutes later with two large suitcases. "I'll get the rest of my things later. You should get a lawyer of your own. I want this signed and over quickly. The kids are grown, so we won't have any custody hassles. Let's just get this signed and move on."

She sat there as the night darkened without even reading the papers on the table. Then she got up, dumped dinner in the trash, and headed to the sunroom, her favorite spot in the house. She curled up in her chair and fell asleep. But the next morning when she woke up, reality hit her. Victor had left. The kids were grown, moved out, and didn't need her. She was alone. And suddenly she had no idea of who she was.

Maxine shook her head, chasing away the memories. There was no use spoiling a perfectly fine evening with thoughts of what had happened. She couldn't change it. Victor had left. She was on her own now. She just had to make the best of it. And she would. Coming back to Magnolia Key had been the first step.

Although she still had no idea of who she was anymore...

CHAPTER 5

Promptly at three the next day, Dale showed up with the bookcase in the back of his delivery van. He used a dolly to bring it in and put it in the storage room.

"I really like the lines, and I think it's going to be the perfect size." Beverly stood back, eyeing it.

"I do, too. I can't wait to get started painting it."

"The general store has some paint here on the island, but you'd have a better selection on the mainland. I'm headed over there to the big hardware store on Monday if you want to tag along and pick out what you need," Dale offered.

Maxine looked at Beverly. "Would that be okay, or do you need me to work?"

"No, that's fine. Besides, you'd be doing me a favor to get this all painted and finished."

"I'm taking the ten o'clock ferry. I could pick you up, then we'd only have the one vehicle."

"That will work." Maxine couldn't wait to get started on the project. She just hoped it turned out as great in reality as it did in her mind.

"I've got to go do some paperwork. I'll see you back at home." Beverly turned and headed into her office.

Dale stood there shifting from foot to foot. "So… I guess that's all you need?"

"Yes, thank you. It was so nice of you to deliver it too."

"I didn't mind." He shifted again and gave a little smile.

Silence fell between them. She searched for something to say. "So, you took over Ginger's shop for her?" Of course he did. That was obvious.

"I did. Helped her out when I first got to town. She still insisted on coming to work each day, even after her fall. Slowly she cut back on how much she worked until…"

"I was sorry to hear of her passing. She was a great lady. Always let me browse around in her store, and she found special items she knew I'd be interested in. I still have a small wooden box I got from there. It has a carved tree on the lid. So pretty. It had a broken hinge, so she let me have it for a big discount." She laughed. "Then she helped me fix the hinge."

"Sounds like my aunt. She always wanted each item to go to someone who would appreciate it." Sadness lurked in the depths of his eyes.

"You must miss her."

"I do. We were so close. She was the last living member of my family."

"Oh, I'm sorry. That must be hard."

"I'm just glad I moved to Magnolia when I did, so I had all those years with her. Besides, I really love living here. Love how everyone is so friendly. And it's a slower pace than the life I had back in San Francisco."

"I bet that was a change for you. I'm finding it quite different from my life back in Philadelphia too."

"I heard you were originally from here in Magnolia. What made you move back?"

Not really a question she knew how to

answer. At least not without getting into the messy details of her divorce and her failed attempts at finding a job back home. She wasn't about to tell him all about that. So she just said, "I needed a change. A fresh start."

"Magnolia Key is a good place for that. It sure gave me a much-needed change."

He didn't expound on why he'd needed a change either, and she didn't press him.

He shoved the bookcase a bit closer to the window. "I heard you're staying with Beverly."

"I am. At least for a bit. And it's fun catching up with her. We were best friends growing up here. Always together." She gave a little laugh. "And I guess we're right back to that now. Working together and living together."

He glanced at his watch. "Well, I better run. Have another delivery, then I'll head back to the store."

"Thanks again for the help."

"Come by the store anytime to browse if you like." He gave her a quick smile and a nod and left the room.

He really was a nice guy. Friendly. Helpful. She probably would take him up on his offer and go browse around his shop again. She did enjoy that. Not because she'd see him again if she went…

Shaking her head at her thoughts, she walked over to the bookcase and smiled. Such big plans for this piece of furniture. Ginger would have been happy to see it go to such good use.

Later that evening, Beverly and Maxine strolled over to the town park with two camp chairs. They set up not far from the gazebo. Soon more townspeople showed up and milled around, waiting for the barbershop quartet to begin.

"Ladies, good evening." Dale walked up to where they were sitting. "Mind if I join you?"

"No, of course not. Sit." Beverly smiled at him. She noticed he placed his chair next to Maxine's. Good. Maybe the two of them would hit it off. Maxine needed more friends here in Magnolia. And she needed some outside interests besides just working at Coastal Coffee.

She enjoyed having her friend back here in town. It was almost like old times. Except they worked instead of studied and had way less free time. She still felt like there was a distance between them though. But maybe that was normal after so long. They'd spent so many years apart.

"Look. There's Miss Eleanor." Maxine leaned close and nodded toward the edge of the crowd.

"She does like it when the town holds events here at the town park. That's why she's always spearheading a fundraiser for it. To keep the park nice and raise money for things like the barbershop quartet and festivals."

"I really do need to volunteer for the fundraiser." Maxine frowned. "When is it?"

"It's next weekend."

"Maybe I should run over there and tell her I'll help."

Just then, the quartet took the stage. "Maybe afterward," Beverly whispered.

Soon the men were singing in perfect harmony. They got the crowd to sing along on some of their songs, and she thoroughly enjoyed their concert.

"That was great. I'd forgotten how much fun concerts in the park were." Maxine stood at the end and closed up her chair.

"They are fun. I'm glad we caught this one." Beverly stood.

"I'm going to see if I can catch Miss Eleanor and let her know I'll help with her fundraiser."

"Here, I'll go with you," Dale said. "I've been meaning to volunteer too."

"I'll catch you later at home. I want to run by the shop." Beverly didn't really need to go by the shop but figured she'd give Maxine and Dale some time together. Never hurt to give people a gentle push.

Oh, look at her. Trying to be the matchmaker. She shook her head at herself as she slung the chair strap over her shoulder.

"Okay, see you back at the cottage." Maxine nodded before turning and heading over toward Eleanor.

CHAPTER 6

Dale walked beside Maxine as they headed across the grassy area, over to where Eleanor was standing. Maxine put on a wide smile as she approached. "Miss Eleanor. I wanted to volunteer for the fundraiser next weekend. Saturday, right?"

Eleanor eyed her. "Yes. I wondered if you were going to help out or not."

"I… uh… of course I want to help." She struggled to keep from flinching as Eleanor frowned at her.

"I'd like to help out too." Dale stepped in and offered. "I can help set up, or whatever you need."

"We're setting up at eight a.m. sharp on

Saturday. We need tables set up for the silent auction. And we'll have the bake sale, of course."

"I'll be there right at eight," Dale assured her.

Eleanor turned to her, and her eyes narrowed into a quizzical look. "And I need someone to run the bake sale table. Handle the cash. Do you think you can manage that?"

"Yes, ma'am." Maxine was certain Miss Eleanor still pictured her as some ten-year-old girl incapable of handling any responsibility.

"Good. I expect you both at eight." Eleanor gave them both a stern look. She squared her shoulders, turned, and headed away, her stride slow but steady as she moved.

"I guess a thank you was a little too much for her," Maxine said under her breath as she watched Eleanor walk over to the sidewalk, surprisingly spry for her age. She turned to Dale, who was grinning at her. "Oh, I guess you heard that. Not very nice of me. She *is* organizing the whole fundraiser. She just needs volunteers."

"Miss Eleanor is…" He shrugged. "I don't even know how to describe her. But she gets things done."

"That she does. Though she makes me feel like I'm a kid."

"She does that to me too. I've learned to live with it." He laughed. "Here, let me take your chair and I'll walk you home."

"You don't have to do that."

"I'd like to," he insisted as he took her chair and flung the carrying strap over his shoulder. "And Beverly's house is on the way to mine."

"Okay, in that case, thank you." When was the last time a man had walked her home? Not that it meant anything. He was just being nice. Friendly. Welcoming her to town.

They headed down the sidewalk toward Beverly's, he pointed out interesting things along the way. A new shop that had gone in on Main Street at the beginning of the year. The new windows in city hall. A large poinciana tree that had weathered the last hurricane, much to the surprise and delight of everyone.

"You seem to know everything that's happening here in Magnolia." She slowed down as they got in front of Beverly's house.

"It's a small town. Everyone knows everything." He shrugged.

"I'd forgotten about that. It's sure hard to keep anything secret here in Magnolia."

He shook his head and gave her a grin. "I wouldn't even try."

She took her chair from him. "Thanks for the company on the walk home."

"My pleasure." He nodded.

"Well… good night then." She stood there awkwardly. "I should go in."

"Yes. Good night. I'm sure I'll see you around."

She headed inside and flipped on the light. She glanced out the window to see him heading off down the sidewalk, the strap of his chair slung across one of his broad shoulders.

It had been a nice evening. And Dale's company on the walk home had been unexpected and… enjoyable.

He was just being friendly, she reminded herself.

Dale headed down the sidewalk, the balmy night air his only company. He'd had a good time at the park this evening. It had been nice sitting with Beverly and Maxine.

Okay, really nice sitting next to Maxine. She

was the first woman in a long time to catch his eye. She was friendly, funny, and hardworking. And he loved that she was fixing up the bookcase to help Beverly.

He wondered what it would be like to have a friend you'd known since childhood and were still friends with. His parents had moved him around so many times when he was a kid. He'd lived in six cities by the time he got to high school, then they'd moved again his senior year. Not much of a chance to make lifelong friends with a childhood like that.

But at least he'd had summers with his aunt. She'd welcomed him every summer for a month-long stay. He helped out at the shop and she taught him how to restore furniture. They'd go for walks on the beach, collecting shells, and get ice cream cones from the ice cream shop. At least he had one constant in his childhood. His aunt. Which is why when she took a fall, he came to help her out. That and the fact the timing was precisely right for him. He'd needed a change. Needed to get away from San Francisco.

He headed up the drive to his aunt's cottage. He still thought of it as hers, but it was his now.

A cute little bungalow on the beach. It had a small guest cottage out back where he'd lived until Aunt Ginger passed away. He'd resisted moving into the main house for months after she was gone. But she'd insisted before she died that he have the house and live there. So he finally did as she wished. He missed her every day. Her smile. The way she sang as she worked in the kitchen. He had friends here, of course. But it just wasn't the same. Some nights, loneliness just seemed to cling to the air in the cottage.

He set his chair on the porch and headed inside, flipping on the light. The warm glow illuminated the main room. He hadn't really changed a thing when he moved in. A couch with large magnolia blooms on it sat against one wall. Wasn't his style, but he couldn't bear to part with it. He looked over at the bookshelves lining one wall. He'd go through them and see if there were some books he could donate to Beverly's lending library. Aunt Ginger had been an avid romance reader. She'd be pleased if others were enjoying her books.

He wandered through the house and stepped out onto the deck, away from the loneliness of the cottage. The moon played hide and seek behind the clouds. It popped out and tossed silver beams of light across the waves. A bird called in the distance. The salty air ruffled his hair. He wasn't sure why he all of a sudden felt out of sorts. But he did. And he wasn't sure how to fix it.

CHAPTER 7

D ale picked Maxine up promptly at nine forty-five on Monday. She climbed into his van and they drove to the ferry landing, joining the short line of vehicles headed for the mainland. The boat approached the landing and let off the arriving cars and people. Soon their line rolled onto the ferry and Dale parked his vehicle.

"You want to head up top? Catch the view on the way over?" he asked as he shut off the motor.

"Yes, let's do that." They headed up the stairs and out onto the top level of the ferry. She watched as the captain cast off, and soon they were chugging their way across the bay. The ferry cut through the water, throwing billowing wake behind them. She laughed as the wind tossed her curls this way and that. She knew better than this. To not bring something to tie her hair back.

"A bit windy up here today." Dale looked at her fighting back her curls.

"It is. But I still much prefer coming up top rather than sitting in the car or in the downstairs waiting area. There's just something about being out on the bay. The view. Seeing the island fade and the mainland grow larger."

Dale pointed off to the side. "And soon, the ferry won't be needed. They say the bridge is planned to be finished sometime next year, though they've had quite a few delays."

"It will be so different after the bridge is in, won't it?"

"It will. Good for business, probably. But I fear it will change the town. I've really gotten into the history of it since I moved here. My aunt knew so much about it and told me a lot of stories. Then I found a few books on the history of the town. And it just grew from there."

"Beverly said you have a section of your store set up as a kind of historical section."

"I do. It's as close as the town will ever get to an actual history museum, I guess." His smile radiated his enthusiasm for learning the history of Magnolia Key. "I want to see if we can preserve the history, and yet, I know the town needs to change with the times. I just don't want everything we love about it to be upended with the bridge."

"I'd love to see your historical collection. Wouldn't mind learning more about the island myself. I mean, I grew up here, but I wasn't interested in old stories back then." She laughed. "I was more interested in boys. Or hanging out with my friends at the beach."

"Did you have a special boyfriend back then?"

"Not really. Dated a few boys, but nothing serious. Then I went away to college, and that's where I met my husband."

Dale looked surprised.

"I mean my ex-husband." It was still hard for her to remember to refer to him as that. "We're divorced. A few years now."

"I'm sorry."

"No, it's fine. I mean, it was hard, but I'm adjusting to it. We have two kids, but they're grown now. They seem to be fine with it all."

Better than she was. But then, they had their lives, their homes, their jobs.

"So you decided to move back here?"

"I did. I needed a fresh start. And Magnolia Key just seemed like the place to try. I'm not sure how long I'll stay, but for now, I'm happy here."

"So, this isn't a permanent move?"

She looked out over the water and frowned. "I don't really know. Haven't thought that far ahead about things. I just needed a place to land. A job. Found both of those things here."

"I'm glad you're here." The corners of his mouth twitched up in a warm, genuine smile.

She wasn't quite sure how to take his remark. Was he just being friendly? Or just thought it was nice that she'd found her footing here? But had she? She was still living with Beverly, not making it on her own. And Beverly refused to let her pay any rent. She did buy lots of their groceries and helped clean and cook. Still, she longed for a place she could call her own.

"We're about at the mainland. Let's go down and get in the van." Dale led the way back downstairs, and they pulled off at the landing. He drove them to a large hardware store.

"This is new since the last time I was home."

"Opened a couple years ago. And there's one of those big warehouse clubs right down the way."

"There were always more choices and places to go when we'd come over here from the island, but not this many. Lots of changes."

Once inside, he helped her pick out the supplies she needed to paint the bookcase. A drop cloth, paint, brushes, sandpaper, and a wax finish to apply as the last step.

He got the things he needed, and they checked out, piling their purchases into the van. "Say, I'm starved. Want to grab something to eat before we head back?" Dale closed the back door of the van.

She nodded. "I'm hungry too."

"There's a new restaurant right near the pier. We could try it. I haven't been yet."

"Sounds good."

He drove them to the pier, and they went into Beachcomber, the new restaurant. They both enjoyed the fish tacos and hushpuppies. The food was delicious and they indulged in easy conversation. He grabbed the check and insisted on buying their lunch.

"You don't have to do that."

"I want to. Enjoyed the company."

They headed back to his van and drove to the landing, sitting in line, waiting for the ferry to arrive.

"I appreciate the ride over here. I can't wait to get started on the bookcase."

"I can't wait to see how it turns out."

They sat and chatted as they waited in line. A comfortable conversation that veered this way and that. He was easy to talk to, funny, and a good listener too.

Soon they were back on the ferry and once again went up top. The warm sunshine bathed her face as she turned to the sun. The salty wind surrounded them, keeping it from being too warm in the sun. All too soon, they were back at Magnolia Key.

"Let's drop your supplies off at Coastal Coffee."

"Okay, thanks. That will make it easier."

They pulled up just as Beverly was closing up. "There you are. Did you find what you needed?"

"I did." She held up a can of paint and nodded toward Dale, laden with bags of her other supplies. "We'll just take them to the back."

They headed to the storeroom and placed all her supplies by the bookcase. Sun streamed in the window. She turned to Dale. "You know what? I'm going to get started right now. I'm going to do some sanding."

"You are anxious, aren't you?" His lips rose in a grin. "Well, I'll leave you to it, then."

"Thanks for everything. The ride, lunch, the conversation."

"You bet. We'll have to do it again soon." He turned and walked out.

Do what soon? Run errands on the mainland? Or lunch? Spend time together? She stared at the empty doorway where he'd disappeared. Dale was a surprise she hadn't expected when she decided to come back to Magnolia Key.

Maxine paused in the sanding of the bookcase to answer her phone.

"Mom, where are you?"

Maxine winced at the accusing tone of her daughter's voice. "I'm in Magnolia Key."

"You are? Why didn't you tell me?"

"I texted you before I left." Not that Tiffany had answered the text.

"You did? I must have missed it."

Like most of the other texts she sent. She was almost certain her texts to her kids went to some big don't-bother-to-read spam place on their phones.

"When are you coming back? Dad called and he's annoyed. He needs you to come to his office this week and sign something. Some kind of settlement that was pending from your divorce."

Victor being annoyed wasn't her problem anymore.

"Something to do with stocks you both owned. There's a check for you too."

This is exactly the kind of thing she would have handled for Victor when they were married. She'd rush over to sign the paperwork on his time schedule. "He can just mail it to me."

"Can't you come back?"

Seriously? Tiffany was asking her to come

back to sign paperwork on Victor's timeline? Not happening. "Have him send it to me."

"Well, when will you be home?"

"I'm not sure. I'll give you my friend Beverly's address here on Magnolia Key. He can send it there."

"Won't you be home soon? You don't ever stay long when you go visit."

"I'm staying longer this time. Tiff, can you just have him send it? I'll sign it and send it back to him. I'll text you Beverly's address." Tiffany would actually have to check her text this time.

"Dad's not going to be pleased. He thought he could wrap this up right away. Something that has to be signed before he can deposit his check."

"It's the best I can do." And all she would do. She wondered why the rush to have the paper signed, anyway. More likely, it was just that he didn't have control over her anymore. Couldn't make her drive across town to sign when he wanted her to.

"I'll tell him, but he won't be happy."

"Okay, thanks, sweetheart," she said as sincerely as she could.

"Does David know you're in Magnolia?"

"I left him a phone message. Yes." Not that her son had answered her, either.

"Let us know when you come home."

"I will." Not that she had any plans to go back there anytime soon. If ever. But that wouldn't really change her kids' lives much. They rarely made time to see her. It made her feel like a failure as a mother, but she wasn't certain what she would have done differently. She gave them everything they needed, wanted. Spent time with them when they were young. Went to all their activities. Helped with homework. Gave them her unending love and attention.

But in spite of all that, they were just not interested in her life or seeing her often. They had, unfortunately, gotten their father's self-centered attitude. It dug at her heart, and she'd tried really hard the last few years since Victor divorced her to see if she could still make the kids feel like they had a family. She'd failed at that, too.

Sometimes all the little—and big—failures in her life piled up and threatened to smother her.

She realized Tiffany had hung up, and she was just standing there holding her phone. She slipped the phone back into her pocket and picked up the sandpaper block again. Back and forth over the wood in long, soothing strokes. Letting the repetitive motion calm her and push the thoughts of failure far from her mind. She'd make sure this bookcase was perfect so Beverly would be proud of it. And it was going to be used for such a good cause, a town lending library. Maybe it would make her feel like part of the town. Even a little bit. She so longed to feel like she belonged here again.

CHAPTER 8

O n Saturday, Maxine made sure she was
at the town park a bit before eight.
There was no way she was going to risk Miss
Eleanor's wrath by being late. She laughed
when she saw Dale was already there.

He grinned a welcoming smile as she walked
up to him. "I see you're early, too."

"Of course. Since Miss Eleanor doesn't even
think I'm capable of collecting money for the
bake sale, I thought I'd start out by showing how
responsible I am with being on time." Her lips
twitched into a conspiring smile.

Eleanor walked up to them just then and
Maxine guiltily hid her smile, hoping Miss
Eleanor hadn't heard her remark.

"There you are. Dale, the tables are at city hall. In the storage room. You need to use your van to go pick them up and bring them over. We need to get a few of the tables put up quickly. People will start delivering items for the bake sale at nine. We have to have those tables up by then."

"Yes, ma'am."

Eleanor eyed him. "What are you waiting for?"

He sent a wink Maxine's way as he hurried off to do as he was told.

"Maxine, you'll set up the baking table. Try to sort the items by what they are. Pies together, cookies together, breads together. You can handle that?" Eleanor tilted her head, eyeing her.

"Yes, I've got it." She hoped she sorted everything up to Eleanor's standards.

When Dale returned with a load of tables, she wrestled with ones for the bake sale while he set some up across the park for the silent auction. She struggled with the last table and thought she had the legs firmly in place, but it collapsed right when Eleanor walked up to her.

"Do I need to make sure you know how to

set up the tables?" Eleanor frowned. "We can't have them falling over and all the baked goods ruined."

"No, I've got it." Her cheeks heated up from embarrassment. She worked on the leg again under Eleanor's watchful eye, this time assuring it was locked into place. She pushed against the table, showing Eleanor that it was all set up and sturdy this time.

Eleanor bobbed her head once, still frowning, and hurried away.

People started to come and deliver items for the sale. Beverly arrived with pots of coffee and hot chocolate, and she set up near the bake sale. She was donating all the profits to the fundraiser.

Soon, the park filled with people milling around. Miss Eleanor watched over the whole proceedings like a hawk. By the end of the day, they'd exceeded their fundraising goal.

Eleanor stood by the chalkboard easel and wrote the final tally. The crowd clapped as she turned around, and a rare smile crossed her features. "Thank all of you for making this a successful fundraiser."

The amount they raised surprised Maxine

and yet it didn't. The town had always rallied around a good cause.

As the people wandered away, Maxine and Dale began taking down the tables. Eleanor approached them. "Thank you, both of you, for your help."

Maxine tried to hide her surprise at the thanks. "You're more than welcome. It went to a good cause."

"Now, Dale. I hear you're handy with a hammer and saw. Now that we have the funds, I'm hoping to do some needed repairs on the gazebo. Then it will need a fresh coat of paint. You'll volunteer to do that." It was more of a statement than a question.

"Yes, ma'am. I'd be glad to."

Eleanor nodded as if it never occurred to her that he wouldn't.

Beverly walked up to them. "Dale, glad I caught you. I've been meaning to show you something. I found a rolled-up painting hidden in the built-in bookcase in my office. Isn't that strange?"

Eleanor choked a bit, her eyes widening before a non-committal look settled back on her features.

"You okay?" Maxine asked.

"Of course." She nodded, dismissing Maxine's concern.

"I could come by and look at it," Dale offered.

"It's pretty old, I think. And it's so strange. It's not a painting of Magnolia Key, but there's an old building on it. It looks exactly like the one we used to have here by the landing. And that hasn't been here for over fifty years. The building didn't look that old in the painting either. I thought with your knowledge of antiques and things, you might have some idea of when it was painted and maybe who painted it. Or maybe even an idea of the location depicted in the painting. Just seems strange it was hidden here, doesn't it?"

"I'll come by this week to see it."

"Thank you. It does have my curiosity going."

"Enough talk about the painting," Eleanor interrupted. "Are you going to finish with the cleanup?"

"Of course," Dale said, shooting Maxine a quick look of amusement. "We're on it."

Eleanor then turned and walked away.

"Miss Eleanor had a strange reaction when you mentioned the painting." Maxine frowned.

"Maybe." Beverly's brow creased. "I should show it to her."

"Good idea. She knows a lot about the town's history too," Dale said. "And it is strange that the exact same building is in the painting."

"Or maybe I'm imagining that. But there is just something about the building that makes me think it's exactly like our old landing building."

"I'll pull some old photos of it and check," Dale offered.

"That would be great. I've got to get my things back to Coastal Coffee. The coffee urn and stuff. You guys good here?"

"We've got this," Dale said.

They took the last of the tables down and loaded them into Dale's van. "Well, that was a full day. I was glad the town came out in support. Miss Eleanor looked pleased with the total funds raised, didn't she?"

"She did. I swear she almost smiled."

"I saw that." He closed the door on the van. "I should get these back to city hall."

"You need help?"

"No, I've got it."

He climbed in, gave a small wave, and pulled away. She stood there on the sidewalk, watching the van head down the road. It was good to feel like part of the town today. To help in raising money for the park. She hummed under her breath as she headed back toward Beverly's cottage.

CHAPTER 9

On Tuesday morning Eleanor came in as usual and sat at her table. Maxine brought her coffee but was reprimanded when she didn't bring cream over with it. Maxine motioned to the bowl of creamers on the table.

"Not that fake stuff. I always use real cream. Beverly brings it to me in a nice little pitcher."

She hurried to the kitchen to do as Miss Eleanor instructed. "Beverly? Miss Eleanor is here. She—"

"Needs her cream." Beverly smiled as she held out the pitcher. "None of those little creamer cups for her."

"Thanks." She'd have to remember Miss Eleanore's quirks. Maxine hurried back out and delivered the requested cream to Miss Eleanor's table.

"I'll have the blueberry muffin. And Beverly always heats it up for me."

"Yes, ma'am." Another thing to remember.

She brought out Miss Eleanor's food and took the orders from two more tables. Janine came walking out from the kitchen, and the tray of food she was carrying tilted precariously. Thankfully, the girl managed to get everything to the table unscathed.

"Hey there."

She whirled around at the sound of Dale's voice, and her lips slipped into a spontaneous smile. "Good morning."

"I thought I'd grab breakfast and take a peek at the painting Beverly found."

"Great. Just grab a table. I'll let her know you're here."

They returned to his table with the painting. "Here it is," Beverly said. "I can't see a signature on it."

Dale looked it over carefully. "I'd say it's at least a hundred years old. Maybe a bit older, I'm guessing, from the age of the building here. Looks like it's fairly new at the time of the painting. And the boats look like they're from about that era, too."

"I wonder if Eleanor might have any clues. Let's show it to her," Beverly said.

The three of them headed over to Miss Eleanor's table. She looked up at them, clearly not pleased at the interruption. "Yes?" Her brow creased in a frown.

"That painting I mentioned finding, I have it here." Beverly held it out to her. "Could you look at it and see if you might have any idea on who painted it? It's the same building that we used to have at the landing, but it's not of Magnolia Key. Any ideas?"

Eleanor signed, looking annoyed, but took the painting. She glanced at it for a moment and the briefest flicker of something crossed her features. Maxine tried to decipher what the look was, but it was gone too quickly.

"I really have no idea." Eleanor gaze slid over to the other painting Beverly had on her wall and then she quickly looked back at the one she was holding. "No idea at all."

Maxine swore Eleanor wasn't telling the whole truth. But why? What was she hiding?

"Now, if you don't mind, I'd like to get back to my meal."

"Of course." Beverly took the painting. "Sorry to bother you."

Miss Eleanor gave them a dismissive nod and they headed back to Dale's table.

"I feel like she's not telling us something." Beverly frowned.

"You got that feeling too? So did I. But why wouldn't she tell us if she knows something?"

"I have no idea." Beverly shook her head.

"I could frame the canvas for you if you want to put it up here at Coastal Coffee," Dale said.

"I'd love that. And who knows, maybe someone who comes in will have some idea of who painted it or where the location is. Thank you." Beverly started to walk away. "Oh, and breakfast is on me. And Maxine, it's time for your break. Why don't you join Dale?"

"You sure?"

Beverly nodded. As she walked away, a small smile spread across her face.

"How about you tell me what you want for breakfast, and I'll go get it?" Maxine glanced at Dale.

"Whatever the muffin is today, and some coffee. And you'll join me?"

"I will."

She returned with their food and sat across from him, enjoying a moment off her feet. "That was nice of you to offer to frame the painting. Maybe Beverly is right and someone who comes in will know more about it."

"Hope so. I'm going to look at some old photos of the landing too. See if it really is an exact copy of the building we had." He smiled. "I do love a bit of a historical mystery. The history of this island fascinates me. Like why did someone pick this particular island to settle on? What made them want to live here? And there appears to be some discrepancy on whether Belle Island or Magnolia Key was settled first. Though it appears both were settled at about the same time."

"But Belle Island got a bridge. They've had it for a long time."

"They are closer to the mainland, though. It makes sense." Dale glanced at the painting again. "I guess it was inevitable that eventually we'd get a bridge too. But I'd like to preserve the legacy and traditions of Magnolia Key, even if we do have big changes coming with our bridge."

"But at least you'll still have Second Finds. That won't change. I mean..." She frowned. "You're planning on keeping the shop, right?"

"I am. I feel like it honors my aunt's memory. She loved the shop." He shrugged. "And so do I. I love being immersed in all that history. I often wonder how some items end up there."

"I can't imagine being able to be in there all day, every day. It must be wonderful. I swear I could live in a shop like that. I've always loved antiquing and visiting thrift shops." She loved the smell of them, the thrill of finding just the right item.

"Like I said before, you're welcome to come in any time."

"I will. I'll come by soon." She glanced over as the door opened and two groups of people came in. "I should really get back to work. Looks like we're going to have a late morning rush." She stood up reluctantly.

"Thanks for joining me. And I guess I'll see you soon." He gave her a warm smile. But then he was a friendly man. It probably wasn't any special smile just for her.

She hurried over to greet the customers and soon was busy working. She didn't even notice when Dale left and tried not to let her feelings be hurt that he hadn't said goodbye. That was silly anyway. He didn't have to say goodbye. He was just here to see the painting and have breakfast. Not to see her.

CHAPTER 10

Maxine worked on the bookcase in her spare time over the next week or so. Sanding, painting, applying a light glaze that highlighted the carvings at the top of the bookcase, then finally rubbing in a wax finish. She ran her fingers along the shelves, loving the feel of the wax on the freshly painted wood.

Sal helped her wrestle the bookcase to its spot on the wall while Beverly was out running errands one morning. When Beverly returned, she exclaimed in delight, "Oh, it's wonderful. Better than I could have imagined. And look how it brightens up that corner of the room."

"We just need some books and a sign and we're all set." Maxine stood back, admiring her handiwork and beaming with pride at Beverly's approval.

Beverly tilted her head. "That top shelf is pretty high. Maybe we should put some decorations on it instead of books."

"That's a good idea."

Beverly's lips twitched into a grin. "Glad you like the idea because I'm putting you in charge of getting something to go up there."

Maxine laughed. "Okay then. Beach decor or maybe…" She paused and looked at the shelf. "Maybe some old-time items? Something that speaks to the history of the island?"

"I love that idea. Just a few small things. I bet you could find something like that at Second Finds."

"I bet I could."

"No time like the present." Beverly nudged her.

Maxine wouldn't mind going to Second Finds again. She'd only seen Dale once this week when he'd come in for breakfast. He'd stayed a long time, lingering over his coffee, but they'd been so busy she hadn't had much time to chat with him.

"Oh, and this came in the mail for you." Beverly handed her an envelope.

She saw it was from Victor's law firm and opened it slowly, pulling out a legal-looking document and a check. She gasped. "Oh… wow."

Beverly's brow creased. "What is it? Is something wrong?"

"No… it's… look at this check."

She held the check out, and Beverly's eyes widened. "Wow is right."

"I had no idea it was this much."

"That's a nice nest egg."

"It is. It's from some kind of settlement that was tied up during the divorce proceedings. I have to sign the paperwork and then I can deposit the check." Victor sure had kept mum about the amount of the settlement. He'd probably hoped he could sneak it all into his account. Luckily, her part of the settlement had been made out to her name.

She couldn't believe her good fortune. Now she'd have money to put down on a deposit on an apartment, plus more to add to her savings. She'd enjoyed staying with Beverly but couldn't help but feel like Beverly might be missing her alone time.

"I'm going to run by the bank, then over to Second Finds." She could hardly take the goofy grin off her face. Money. A nest egg. *And* a trip to see Dale. Well, a trip to look for items for the bookshelf. That's all it was.

Beverly shook her head and smiled at her. "You have fun. I'll see you later."

Maxine practically danced her way out of Coastal Coffee.

Maxine went to the bank and deposited the check, feeling almost rich. Well, compared to her financial situation for the last few years. It had been scary living without much backup savings. Now she could breathe easier.

Victor had a sharp lawyer handle the divorce and ended up with almost everything. She hadn't been able to afford a top-notch lawyer like his. So she was happy she finally ended up with something to show from their years of marriage and all she'd done to run his life for him so he could concentrate on business. He'd insisted she never get a job while they were married because she needed to be ready at a moment's notice to throw a dinner party or handle anything else that came up that he didn't want to deal with. Not to mention be the one who always handled everything kid related. She wasn't sure how she'd let herself be put in that position, and it annoyed her thinking back on it. But the past was the past, and it was silly to waste time with the what-ifs.

She walked out of the bank and into the sunshine, letting it bathe away her regrets. She turned and headed down the sidewalk to Second Finds, anxious to see what she could find for Beverly's bookcase.

She pushed into the store and smiled as the sound of the bell rang over the door. The familiar scents and sights of the shop greeted her.

Dale looked up from where he was unpacking a box across the room. "Well, hello there."

She crossed over to him. "Hi. Beverly sent me on a mission."

"Oh?"

"I finished the bookcase, but she thinks we should put some historical memorabilia on the top shelf. It's pretty high and I think it would be hard for people to search out books on it."

"You've come to the right place." He swept

his arm out in dramatic fashion. "I happen to have quite a bit of history in here."

"Do you have any suggestions for me?"

"I have some hand-blown fishing net floats. They were used in the 1800s and early 1900s."

"Oh, I like that idea. Very island-y."

"I also have an old ship's porthole that I made a wooden stand for to hold it upright. It's a small porthole, about twelve inches."

"That will fit, and it's another wonderful idea. I'm grateful to have your help with this."

"Here, I'll show them to you."

She followed him deep into the shop and agreed with both his choices. "I think I'll wander around a bit more and see what else I can find."

"Of course. Stay as long as you like. I'll take these two items up to the checkout."

She wandered around the store, getting lost in the history. Old leather suitcases, vintage clothing, more old paintings. Then she found an old handbag and white gloves. That would be perfect.

She carried them up to the front of the store. "Look at these. I love the intricate beading on the purse."

"I would guess that's from the 1920s. It's in nice shape. And those long white gloves are called opera gloves. They were very fashionable during that same era."

"I think they will be perfect. A bit of nautical and a bit of women's fashion."

"You made great choices." Dale rang up the purchase. "I'll deliver them tomorrow, if that's okay. The porthole is heavy."

"Okay, thank you. But I think I'll take the purse and gloves with me." She would have liked to stay longer and just browse, but she'd already been here for over an hour.

"I—uh…" Dale looked at her for a moment. "I was wondering. I mean, I was just getting ready to close up the shop. Would you like to come over to my place and pick out some books from my aunt's collection? I'd love to donate some to the lending library."

"Yes, I'd love to." And then she'd get to spend more time with him.

Another one of those unexpected thoughts… Where were they coming from?

"Great, I'll just lock up and flip the sign to closed."

They headed outside as he pulled the door

shut behind them. "Walking okay? Or we can take the van."

"Walking is fine."

"Ginger's cottage is this way," Dale said as they headed down the sidewalk, then he laughed. "Oh, I guess you know that. You grew up here. And yes, it's my cottage now. It's just hard to think of it as that."

It was a quick walk just down the street and over to the beach. They climbed the stairs and he let them inside. Late afternoon sunlight streamed in through the windows. He set his keys on the table. "I know what you're thinking. This isn't my style with the floral couch and everything. But I just haven't been able to make myself change anything."

"I don't blame you. And I think it's wonderful. Homey."

"The bookcase is over there." He pointed to the far wall.

She went over and looked at shelf after shelf of books. "She was quite a reader, I guess."

"She was. But take as many as you want. My books are just on that one lower shelf."

She slowly perused the titles and chose about a dozen books. Some romances. A mystery or two. A few classics like Tom Sawyer and Anne of Green Gables. She turned to find Dale watching her.

He smiled guiltily. "Oh, I'm sorry. I just enjoyed watching your face as you chose the books. I take it you're a reader, too?"

"I am. But my favorite books are back in storage in Philadelphia. Though, I'm thinking of getting my own place now, so I'm hoping to get my things sent here."

"So you're going to stay?" His eyes lit up.

"For the foreseeable future, at least. I'm going to look for a small place. Close enough to walk to work at Coastal Coffee."

"I... I have an idea." He paused and chewed his lower lip. "I mean... the small guest cottage behind Ginger's house is empty. I lived in it before moving in here. It's small. Just one bedroom, bath, and a kitchen. Do you want to see it?"

Her heart leapt at the suggestion. "Yes, I'd love to."

She followed him outside and across a small courtyard to the guesthouse. They climbed the front steps and went inside. "Oh, this is wonderful." Warm light flooded the main room, which was a combination family room, kitchen, and breakfast nook.

"The bedroom is back that way."

She went down the hall and peeked into the bedroom. It was also light and had a nice-sized attached bathroom. She turned around to face him. "This is perfect. How much is the rent?" She hoped she could afford it. It *was* right here near the beach.

He laughed. "I have no idea. It just sits here empty now. Enough to cover the utilities would be fine."

"No, that's not enough. And it's right here near the beach. You could get good rent money for it."

"But I'm picky about who lives so close." He winked and a strange warmth settled over her cheeks, which she tried to ignore.

"But I need to pay rent. I need to… make it on my own."

She was pleased to see understanding in his eyes, and they agreed on a number at her insistence.

"I was going to donate most of the furniture in here, but you're free to use what you'd like," he said.

"That would be great until I can get my things sent here."

"You can decorate it how you like. We can paint the rooms if you want."

"You're being an awfully nice landlord," she teased, trying to ignore his twinkling eyes. Happiness bubbled through her at her good fortune today.

"When would you like to move in?"

She grinned. "Is tomorrow too soon?"

"Not at all." He handed her the key.

Excitement sent her pulse racing, and her mind spun with to-do lists. Her own place. And it was so cozy and wonderful and near work.

And near Dale.

But she'd have to make sure she didn't bother him. She'd be the best tenant ever.

"I'm really excited about this move. I can't wait to tell Beverly. She never complains, but I'm sure she'll like to have her space back. I'll move in tomorrow after the coffee shop closes. Thank you so much for this."

"My pleasure. Seems a shame to just let this sit here empty."

They headed back out to the courtyard between the cottages. "I should go now. I have to tell Beverly about this and get to packing up my things."

"I guess I'll see you tomorrow, neighbor." He grinned and reached out to shake her hand.

She took his hand in hers, amazed at the warmth and strength of his grasp. "Tomorrow then… neighbor." She smiled as she turned and headed to Beverly's.

CHAPTER 11

The next morning, Maxine arrived early to Coastal Coffee. In her excitement about today's move, she hadn't been able to sleep much. She'd packed up her things last night and loaded her car this morning before coming into work.

As she unlocked the door at opening time, Nash Carlisle greeted her. "Morning, Maxine. Going to be a hot one today." He grabbed a copy of the paper and went to his usual table. Her work routine neatly dropped into place as she waited on customers and cleared tables, all the while glancing at her watch, anxious for the end of her shift.

As the morning rush died down, she unloaded the box of books Dale had donated and placed them on a shelf. Then she put up the porthole and glass float on the top shelf. He'd dropped them off in the middle of the rush, so she didn't get a chance to thank him again.

Beverly walked over and handed her a carefully lettered sign. Lending Library. They hooked it on a shelf and stood back. "So, it's a beginning," Beverly said. "I'll be sure to mention it to the customers when they come in. See if they have any books to donate or want to borrow one."

"Oh, and I still have a few more things to put up." Maxine reached into the box and pulled out the purse. "Isn't this purse wonderful? So much detail in the beading."

"That is nice."

"Dale said he thinks it's from the 1920s. It's not very big, but I can just picture someone all dressed up for a party back then and carrying this purse, can't you?" She opened it and looked inside. "The lining has a little rip in it." She frowned as she fingered the tear, feeling something rustle beneath the lining.

"What's wrong?" Beverly leaned closer to take a look.

"I think there's… something in here." She carried it over to the window light. "I think there's a piece of paper in here." She chewed her lip. "Oh, it's not a rip. This seam isn't sewn closed. There's an opening."

She carefully slipped her fingers in and felt the mystery object again. She wiggled a yellowed piece of paper out and unfolded it. "Look, it's a letter."

Beverly peered over her shoulder.

"It doesn't make much sense." She narrowed her eyes, trying to decipher all the words. Some were too faded with age to read. "The words I can make out seem a bit disjointed. And there are some numbers here too. It's signed with just a 'V.'"

"I wonder why it's in the purse and who V is?" Beverly took the paper and stared at it. "You're right, it's pretty faded. And it has that old-fashioned handwriting. The kind you see on old census records and things like that."

"I guess this purse must have been the V person's?"

"Or V gave the letter to someone, and this is that someone's purse," Beverly countered.

"It's all very mysterious, isn't it?"

"It's a bit strange how these mysterious items are popping up now, isn't it? Like the hidden painting, and now this?" Beverly's brow creased. "I wonder if we should frame this and put it up on the wall too. Maybe someone in town will have an idea."

"That's a good idea." She put the purse and gloves up on the top shelf and arranged everything so it looked perfect. "I think we're all set now. We've officially opened the lending library."

"Thanks for all your help with it."

"I've loved helping you with it. And working here. And staying with you. I really appreciate all you've done for me." Maxine hugged Beverly. "You really are a great friend."

"I'm going to miss you at the cottage. It's been fun having you stay with me. But I understand how you want to have your own place. I'm happy for you."

"Thanks. I can't wait to get settled in."

The door to the shop opened and a couple groups of customers filed in. "It's back to work time." Beverly headed over to greet them.

Maxine took one last look at the shelf and hurried over to help.

Dale watched the clock all morning at the shop. The minutes seemed to drag by. He wanted to be sure to get back home early so he could help Maxine move into the cottage. Well, if she wanted his help. She did seem to like to do things herself. Have her independence. He guessed that was logical after her divorce. She hadn't said much about it. He didn't know if it had been an amicable one or a nasty one. All he knew was it had been a few years ago. And she had kids, but she didn't talk about them much. There was probably more to the story, but he didn't want to pry.

At two o'clock, he left his employee to handle the shop and headed home after first stopping at the market to pick up a few things for dinner. He put the groceries away, all the while glancing out the window to see if Maxine had arrived.

Finally, he heard her pull into the drive. He popped outside and waved as she climbed out of her car. Her hair was blowing madly in the strong breeze coming off the gulf. She yanked it back away from her face, a movement he was growing accustomed to and it brought an easy grin to his face.

He walked over to the car. "I thought I could help you move your things in."

"You don't have to do that." She swung a suitcase out of the car. "I can get it."

"But I'd love to help."

After a brief pause, she nodded. "Okay, thank you."

They unloaded her car, putting most of her things in a pile in the main room.

"I'll sort through everything in a bit."

She stood there looking at him. Did that mean she wanted him to leave? Or help? Or... what?

"Can I do anything else to help?" he finally asked.

"No, I'm fine. I'm just going to settle in."

"Okay, I'm just across the courtyard if you need anything." He couldn't think of any other reason to delay, so he walked over to the door. "I'll see you soon."

"Yes. And thanks so much for everything. For renting me this cottage and for the help hauling everything in." She glanced at the pile of her belongings, and he got the distinct feeling that, yes, she wanted him to leave.

"My pleasure." He left her to it and returned to his cottage.

Maybe he should have asked her to come have dinner. She probably didn't have anything to eat over there.

Or maybe that would be bothering her. Maybe she just needed time to unpack and settle.

Since when did a woman make him so unsure of himself?

Oh, he knew the answer to that. And the last time had been years and years ago—when he'd learned his lesson and left San Francisco with his heart and his ego in his hands. He should remember that lesson now and give Maxine her space. Not get tied up with a woman who was clearly wanting to make it on her own.

Maxine slowly turned around in the cottage, a smile spreading wide across her face. She flung out her arms and spun around. This was hers. Her own place. Not some cold mansion that Victor picked out. Not some crummy one-room apartment back in Philadelphia, which she hated. She loved this cottage. The light streaming in. Everything about it.

She busied herself unpacking her things,

putting everything away. Hanging clothes in the large closet and putting things in the chest of drawers Dale left here. Thank goodness the bed he left here was a queen-sized one, because she had sheets for that. She made up the bed, put her things away in the bathroom, and hung up some old towels she'd brought with her. She was going to replace those as soon as possible. And get a pretty new bedspread.

Beverly had insisted she take a small box of food items, which she unloaded into the pantry. She'd go shopping for groceries tomorrow. When she looked out the kitchen window, the small view of the ocean delighted her. An unexpected perk.

She sat at the table and opened her laptop. After thirty minutes, she'd made arrangements for her things in storage to get shipped here. Luckily, there was a staging lot right by the ferry landing on the mainland that people used when they were moving to the island or getting larger items delivered. As soon as she was notified that her things had arrived, she would use a local company that would load everything into a small van and deliver them to the island.

After her personal items got here, she'd better know what she needed to get for the cottage. She flipped the laptop closed and walked over to the pantry. She reached in and grabbed some microwave popcorn. That would do for her dinner.

As her dinner cheerily popped in the microwave, she opened a bottle of wine she'd brought. Thankfully, Dale had a wine opener in the drawer.

She walked outside with her bowl of popcorn and glass of wine and settled into one of the Adirondack chairs in the courtyard. This, this was heaven. Her own place. A nice sea breeze coming in from the gulf. The beginning of the sunset. A view of the ocean across the courtyard.

She never would have thought a month ago that her life could turn around like this. A nice job and a great place to live. Renewing her friendship with Beverly. And new friends like Dale. A bit of pride swept through her. She had real hopes of making it on her own now.

She let out a long breath of air. Contentment spilled through her. She leaned back in the chair, balancing the bowl on her lap. She raised her glass to the sky and toasted. "To new beginnings."

CHAPTER 12

Beverly missed having Maxine at her cottage. It seemed so quiet there now. But she had to admit that she did like having her privacy again. Having what she wanted for dinner, when she wanted it. Not worrying that she was waking Maxine if she got up extra early. She was used to living on her own. And she saw Maxine almost every day at Coastal Coffee, of course.

Maxine seemed to be settling into her new life here on Magnolia Key. She was happier these days.

Beverly stirred a huge pot of soup, thinking it was a little too warm of a day for soup, but her customers clamored for it when they didn't serve it at lunch.

Just then, Maxine walked into the kitchen, carrying a tray of dishes. "Nash just left. He had the strawberry muffins. I swear those are his favorite. His eyes light up when he sees them listed on the chalkboard as the day's offering. And Eleanor just came in. I'll need her pitcher of cream."

Beverly laughed as she got the cream from the refrigerator. "You're learning all the customer's quirks, aren't you?"

"I guess I am." A pleased smile swept over her face.

"If Eleanor is here, why don't I go get that letter from my office and we'll show it to her. Maybe she'll know something about it." Beverly dried her hands on a towel.

"Like she probably knows something about that painting you found, but won't tell us?" Maxine shook her head. "I know she's hiding something.

"Maybe we read her wrong. Maybe she didn't know anything about it." Though Beverly didn't think they'd both been wrong about Eleanor's reaction.

She went into the office, retrieved the letter, and headed over to Eleanor's table where Maxine was pouring coffee. "Miss Eleanor,

Maxine found this letter in an old purse she got from Second Finds. Could you take a look at it?"

"Why?" Eleanor eyed them both suspiciously.

"We just thought you might have an idea of who wrote it," Maxine said. "You know a lot about the town's history."

Eleanor sighed, a frown deepening on her brow, and held out her hand. "Let me see it."

Beverly handed her the letter and watched her face carefully. She'd swear a bit of color drained from Eleanor's face, then two tiny patches of red highlighted her cheeks. Eleanor carefully folded the letter.

Eleanor cleared her throat as she handed the letter back. "No. I have no idea who wrote that. Most of it is too faded to read anyway. It doesn't make much sense what you can see."

"Okay, thanks for looking at it." Beverly took the letter. "We're thinking of putting it up on the wall. Maybe someone will know something."

Eleanor's eyes flew open wide. "You can't do that."

"Why not?"

"Well, it's obviously a private letter. Hidden

away so no one would find it. People deserve their privacy."

Eleanor might be right. Maybe it was wrong to post it on the wall. But then, what if they could find out more information about these two mysteries if they did post it up by the painting she'd found? Beverly chewed her bottom lip, wondering if she should do what Eleanor suggested or chance her ire by putting it up and seeing what she could find out.

"So, you'll not post it." It wasn't a request, more like an order. Eleanor didn't give her time to reply before turning to Maxine and double-tapping the table with her fingertips. "Is my muffin ready yet?"

"Coming right up." Maxine hurried away, and Beverly followed her into the kitchen.

"So… did you see her face?" Beverly asked.

"I did. I swear that woman is hiding something." Maxine took a muffin from the tray in the oven where they were sitting to warm. "And she sure doesn't want you to put that letter up, does she?"

"No, she was adamant about that. I just can't figure out her reasoning on this. And why wouldn't she tell us if she knew something about either the painting or the letter? These items are from way before she was born, right?" A gnawing feeling crept through her. She was certain Eleanor was lying.

Maxine nodded. "They would be from before she was born."

Beverly sighed. "Maybe we'll find another lead."

"So, should we hang the letter?" Maxine asked.

"I'm not sure…" She wasn't certain if Miss Eleanor was right, and it was a private letter and she shouldn't violate that privacy… or whether she didn't quite have the nerve to go against Miss Eleanor's wishes.

Maxine rearranged the lending library shelves as the lunch crowd died down. She liked the books arranged by subject, but as people came and looked at them or donated some, the books got placed in the wrong place. She laughed at herself over how particular she'd become about the library, but she couldn't help herself. She like order.

She grabbed the copy of Tom Sawyer that had been Dale's aunt's and placed it by the classics. She hadn't seen much of Dale since she moved into the guest cottage. He'd waved to her from across the courtyard a few times. That was it. He hadn't come into Coastal Coffee either. Maybe he was regretting his decision to let her move into the cottage?

Somehow, she thought they might become better friends after she moved in. Maybe share a meal. Maybe find time to have a drink watching the sunset. And where he'd been eager to offer help about so many things before—but she really did like to do things for herself—now he hadn't even come over to check on her and see how she was faring.

Maybe she'd read him wrong before. Maybe he was just being nice while she got used to being here in town. And now, he was leaving her alone to settle in and make a life for herself.

Which was exactly what she wanted, right?

"You okay?" Beverly stood as she walked past. "You look… perplexed."

"I'm just sorting the books." She didn't want to spill all her self-doubts to Beverly. Beverly was always so self-assured.

"You do like them in perfect order." She smiled, then headed to her office.

Just then, Judy and Harv McNally walked over. She was grateful she remembered their names immediately this time. "Hello, Judy. Harv."

"Maxine. We heard about the lending library and thought we'd donate a few books." Harv set a small box of books down on the floor by the shelf. Which was good, because then she could sort them where they belonged.

"Oh, this bookcase is nice." Judy ran her finger along a shelf. "Look at the pretty color. And the finish. I love it."

"It's an old bookcase I got at Second Finds. I painted it, put some glaze on it, and waxed it." She had to admit she was proud of how it had turned out.

"It's lovely." Judy's brow furrowed. "Say, do you think you could do that on a piece of our furniture? We have this old coffee table that is so beat up. Harv has repaired it a few times. It's still sturdy. But it's a dark wood. It's from our very first apartment, so I can't bear to get rid of it even though it's in such terrible shape and way too dark for my liking. I'd love for it to be painted a nice, light mint green to fit in better with our furnishings."

"We'd pay you, of course," Harv added

quickly. "I think Judy is right. It would look nice."

"I'd love to." This was unexpected. But a way to earn a bit more money and do something she loved to do.

"I could drop off the table. Where would you like me to bring it?"

"I'm not sure... Let me figure something out." Maybe Beverly would let her use the storeroom again because her cottage was crammed full of furniture now and she still had her things being delivered.

"We'll drop by again in a few days and see where you want it. And I'll bring some examples of the shade of mint that I like."

"That would work. Then I'll order in the paint."

"Can you wax it like this bookshelf too? I love that." Judy ran her fingers over the shelf again.

"I can."

"We'll see you soon, then." Harv and Judy walked out of the shop.

Maxine sorted the books into their proper place, then went to find Beverly. She found her in her office. "Hey, guess what? The McNally's came in and Judy wants me to paint a coffee table of theirs."

"Oh, that's great. You like doing that."

"I do. And I was wondering if you'd mind if I used the storage room to do it? I'd do it in my cottage, but my furniture is getting delivered and then Dale wants to donate his furniture. It's going to be a crowded mess for a bit."

"Of course you can."

"Hi, ladies."

Maxine whirled around at the sound of Dale's voice. "Dale…" She didn't really know what to say to him.

"I finished framing the painting you found, Beverly. Thought I'd drop it by."

Beverly rose and walked over to Dale, taking the painting from him. "Oh, that looks nice."

He nodded.

Maxine watched him carefully. He didn't even look her way.

"I'm going to hang it right now."

"I took some photos of it, and I'm still researching to see if I can pin down when it was painted and what it's a painting of." Dale smiled —at Beverly.

"And maybe someone will know something

about it. I just wonder why it was hidden in my bookcase. Who put it there?"

"Right now, it remains a mystery." He shrugged. "I need to get back to the shop."

"Thanks for bringing this over." Beverly smiled at him. "Really appreciate it."

He nodded again and disappeared. Without really saying a word to her—except she guessed she was included in the *hi, ladies*.

Beverly looked over at her. "You okay?"

"I guess so."

"What's wrong?"

"I'm not sure. Dale used to be so friendly. And ever since I moved into his guest cottage, he's been... distant."

"Was he? I didn't notice." Beverly frowned. "Well, maybe a little. He usually lights up when he talks to you."

"No, he doesn't."

Beverly laughed. "Yes. Yes, he does."

"Well, if he did before, he doesn't now. He barely waves to me when he sees me. It's like he's... avoiding me."

"Then why don't you go over and talk to him tonight? Bring a bottle of wine to share or something."

"I don't want to bother him."

Beverly shook her head. "Or maybe he's thinking the very same thing. He doesn't want to bother you. He's giving you some privacy. You should go over."

How had things gotten this complicated? Why was she so unsure of herself? Wasn't she trying to become this more confident woman?

"Maybe I will…" But there wasn't much confidence in her words.

CHAPTER 13

The next morning Maxine woke up early and decided to take a walk to the beach and watch the sunrise. She hadn't been able to sleep very well with Beverly's words rolling around in her head. She'd actually picked up a bottle of wine and started to head over to Dale's last night—twice. But she'd never made it out the door.

She carried her insulated mug of coffee with her to the beach and sat down, watching the birds race around at the frothy edge of the waves. She smiled at their antics.

"Good morning."

She looked up to find Dale standing beside her, coffee mug in hand. "Ah, good morning."

"I don't want to disturb you." He looked at

her tentatively. Or did he look like he wanted to escape?

"You're not. Want to sit down?"

He still looked uncertain.

"Or not. Maybe you want some privacy?" She stared up at him, then frowned. "Are you regretting me moving into the guest cottage?"

His eyes widened. "What? No, of course not."

"My furniture gets delivered today... but if you want, I could look for somewhere else to live."

"Why would you move? I thought you said the guest cottage was perfect."

"It is..." She took a deep breath and pulled up her courage. "But I feel like you've been avoiding me since I moved in. Before that, I thought we were becoming friends."

He dropped down on the sand beside her. "We are friends."

"Then why are you avoiding me?"

"I'm not avoiding..." He laughed gently. "Okay, maybe I have been avoiding you. I just wanted to give you your space. You seem... to want to do things for yourself. On your own."

She stared at him for a moment, then glanced at the birds darting back and forth before answering. "I do want to make it on my own now. I was so dependent on Victor for a lot of things. Mostly to support me. He never wanted me to have a job. I'm not sure how I let him make that decision for me. And... I had a hard time after the divorce. Got fired from some jobs I tried. Lost my house. Well, it never felt like *my* house. It felt like Victor's house. But I ended up in the crummy apartment and..." She stopped, embarrassed she'd spilled all that.

"I'm sorry. That must have been hard."

"I look back on the woman I was and just shake my head. I did everything for Victor and my children. But now... I have nothing to show for it. My kids barely talk to me, no matter how hard I try. It's like my world imploded around me. But now? Now I feel like I've taken back some control. That I'm going to be able to support myself. Make it on my own."

"I'm sure you will." He took a sip of his coffee. "I'll make sure to give you space. I'll quit bothering you with offers of help. You obviously like your newfound independence."

"You aren't bothering me." She paused and gave a small smile. "Okay, you were a bit overwhelming with always offering help. But I...

I like spending time with you. My becoming independent doesn't mean we can't be friends."

He looked at her closely. "I don't want to interfere."

"Dale, where is this coming from? Of course we can still be friends."

He sighed. "I just know when women decide to make it on their own and their independence is the most important thing… Well, then there isn't room for me."

She started to put the pieces together. "So, some woman did that? Broke up with you?"

"Yes. The reason I left San Fransisco. My girlfriend—the woman I dated for over five years and talked to about getting married— decided it wasn't for her. That marriage would hamper her independence. She'd always choose her job and her independence over me."

So that's where he was coming from. His actions made more sense now. She reached out and touched his hand. "Sometimes our past really messes with our future, doesn't it?"

He nodded.

"I do want to make it on my own. I'm proud of how I've started making this life on Magnolia Key work for me." She squeezed his hand. "But

I have lots of room in my life to be friends with you. I *want* to be friends with you."

"And I want to be friends with you." He smiled at her, and the look eased away her confusion on where they stood.

She glanced at her watch. "I'm glad we settled all that. But I need to go. My things should be on the next ferry."

Dale stood and reached down a hand. She took it and he helped her to her feet. "I... uh..." He laughed. "I still don't want to overstep..."

She grinned. "Go ahead. Ask."

"Do you want me to come? I could get some of my things in the cottage out of your way. A few things I think I'll take to Second Finds and sell, and some I'll donate."

"I'd love your help."

A wide smile spread across his face. "Great."

They turned and headed across the sand, and she was glad they'd talked things out. She liked being friends with him. Liked it a lot.

Relief swept through Dale as they headed into the guest cottage. He'd probably overreacted with Maxine. He had to remember not all women were like his last girlfriend. And that had been so many years ago. He'd rarely dated since moving to Magnolia Key. He'd been busy with the shop, of course. And taking care of his aunt. But mostly, he hadn't found a woman who interested him.

At least not until he met Maxine. She interested him.

But he was still going to be careful around her. Not push his help on her. And... take everything slowly, because he still wasn't one hundred percent sure that Maxine wanted anything remotely resembling a relationship.

They went into the cottage and he dragged out some of his furniture, setting it outside to load into his van to take to Second Finds. The men came to deliver Maxine's things, and he kept his opinions to himself about where she should put her furniture. Even when she had them place a large hutch on a wall that was way too small for the piece of furniture. He cheerfully moved it for her without a word when she realized it.

"You know, you can keep any of the furniture that you want," he offered. But then immediately worried he shouldn't have. How did this get so complicated?

"Oh, I couldn't do that. I know you can sell it at Second Finds."

"I see that you don't have a bookcase. I know you're a reader. How about you keep the bookcase?"

"Let me buy it from you."

"You can just have it." He could tell by the strong shake of her head that was the wrong thing to say.

"No, I want to pay for it. And I'd buy the table and chairs off you too. Name a price for all of that." She firmly dipped her head, then smiled. "As long as you don't mind if I paint them."

He started to insist she just take them for free but realized she needed to pay something for them. To feel like she was making it on her own. They agreed on a fair price.

He left to take multiple trips to Second Finds and the donation center, clearing out the rest of his things from the cottage. He returned to find Maxine sitting in the middle of the room, unpacking a box. He stood in the doorway for a moment, watching her, unsure if he should interrupt. Sadness lingered in her eyes as she pulled out a photo album from the box.

He crossed over and knelt down beside her. "Are you okay?"

"Yes. Well, no. Some of this stuff just brings back so many memories. Like these photos from when the kids were little. Victor is in some of them, of course. And I can't erase the past, but it hurts a bit seeing all this history. All the time I put into a relationship that just… fell apart." She sighed. "But it's not like I can just throw these albums away."

"Maybe you could pick out a few photos you want to keep and give the albums to your kids?" he suggested.

She gave a small laugh. "I've already tried to give them things I thought they'd want. Things we had in our house when they were growing up. They didn't want much. Well, my son took a collection of old vinyl albums, but then I found out he just took them to sell them for cash." Pain hovered in her eyes.

"I'm sorry."

"It's just how it all turned out. I wish I could change it—" She frowned. "Maybe I wish I could change how it all turned out. But I can't imagine still being married to Victor. Letting him control my life. I'm not the same person. I couldn't go back to living like that."

"From what I see, you're a survivor. Strong. Independent." *Independent.* That word scared him. Independent meant not needing anyone.

"It's nice of you to say that." She shrugged. "But honestly, I mostly see the failures."

"How about the successes? Starting over again here in Magnolia. A job, a home, friends."

"I still don't really feel like I belong here, though."

"What would make you feel like you do belong?"

She shook her head. "I'm not sure. Everything is just so... different now. It's not how I ever imagined my life turning out. I never thought I'd return to Magnolia."

"Life sometimes throws us curves, doesn't it?"

She nodded slowly. "It does."

"We just have to make the best of it." He reached out and squeezed her hand. "And from where I sit, you *are* making the best of it."

She laughed. "You're sitting on my floor. Which just goes to show, I should probably get a couch."

"You could have kept my old leather one."

"No offense, but it was too heavy and dark

for my taste. I want the place to look light and airy."

"No offense taken. I actually moved it into my cottage. Thought it was time for Aunt Ginger's floral couch to go. Hope she doesn't mind."

"I'm sure she'd just want you to live in a place that felt like home."

Dale stood. "If you don't need me for anything else right now, I need to go close up the shop."

"Yes, go. I appreciate your help today, though."

"My pleasure." He walked to the door and turned back and gave one quick glance at Maxine, sitting on the floor, turning pages of the album. Her face looked a little bit less sad now. Maybe.

CHAPTER 14

Maxine's life settled into a nice routine.
One she enjoyed. Work, redoing
furniture, and spending time with Beverly and
Dale. The coffee table she did for Harv and
Judy turned out beautifully, and when Judy was
bragging about it one day at Coastal Coffee,
another customer asked her to redo a dresser for
her son's room. That was on top of the table,
chairs, and bookcase she did for her own
cottage. Dale complimented the work she did,
unlike Victor, who never complimented her on
anything.

She could tell Dale was still being judicious
with any offers of help. Since they'd cleared up
that misunderstanding, their friendship had

continued to blossom. They took walks on the beach and sat in the courtyard talking, enjoyed the occasional meal together, and often shared wine on his deck while watching the sunset. It was an easy friendship, and a welcome one.

Dale had asked her over for their own happy hour tonight. She brought cheese and crackers and he opened a nice bottle of red wine. They sat outside on his deck, unwinding and chatting about their days. She liked this time they spent together. It's how she'd foolishly imagined—at the beginning of her marriage—she and Victor would have spent their evenings. But that hadn't happened. Victor wasn't interested in her day.

Not the little details that Dale was interested in. Things like what was the special for breakfast. Did anyone new come into Coastal Coffee? How was the lending library going? He always asked questions and seemed genuinely interested in her answers.

"Any more interest in your furniture refinishing?" he asked as he poured them each a glass of wine.

"I did get another job. This one is a cradle that has been in the family for generations. I'm just going to sand it and refinish in a baby-safe stain."

"This side job of yours is really picking up."

"It is. And I enjoy it."

"I was wondering if you'd like to have a small area in my shop to sell some of your refinished furniture. I get a lot of customers wanting more beachy items. We could have a kind of coastal decor corner. We could pick out pieces, you could paint them, and we could split the profits?"

Her pulse raced with excitement from his offer. "I'd love to do that." It was sweet of him to offer her an opportunity like this.

"Perfect. We'll find a day for you to come over and look at some pieces I have in the back storeroom. I have to admit, I was hoping you'd say yes, and I set some pieces aside for you to look at."

This could be a nice source of second income for her. She was always hoping to add to her savings. And it would be fun to work together with Dale. Her mind raced with how they could create a cute corner in his shop full of coastal decor. What colors would go well together to make it all look appealing. What type of furniture. How long it would take to get something like this set up.

He laughed. "I can hear your thoughts rambling around in your brain."

"I'm sorry." She grinned sheepishly. How long had she been lost in her thoughts? "I'm just excited about the idea."

"I am, too. I think it will be profitable for both of us." He raised his glass. "To a new partnership."

She clinked her glass to his, then took a sip, watching him as he did the same. His eyes glimmered with the same excitement she felt.

"I have another question I've been meaning to ask you." He set down his glass and shifted in his chair.

"Oh? What's that?"

"I was wondering. I mean…" He shook his head. "I'm terrible at this. No practice. No clue how to do this right."

"Do what?" What was up with him? He wasn't usually flustered about anything.

"Ask you out. I mean, I'm *trying*—and failing miserably—to ask you out. Will you go out with me? On a date. A real one. You know, we go somewhere together. I pay. We have a good time." He grinned now. "Is that better?"

Surprise crept through her. Though, really, should she be surprised? Didn't she half expect this? Just maybe not this soon. Though she had been here for a few months now.

"So, is that a yes or a no?"

She took a sip of her wine as her surprise faded and was replaced with a growing excitement. "Yes. That's a yes."

"I thought we could go to the mainland and then over to Belle Island. Go to Magic Cafe."

"I haven't been there in years. Seriously, not since I was a teenager. I'd love to go there."

"Perfect. How about Friday?"

"Friday works for me." She was going on a date. How long had it been since she'd gone on a date? So, so many years. Before she'd married Victor. She knew nothing about dating these days. All of a sudden, she was unsure of her answer. What if dating Dale made things awkward between them? What if he decided he wasn't interested in her in that way? Would she lose her friendship with him too? Her heart began to pound, and her pulse quickened. Why did she always have to overthink everything? And saying yes to this date was no exception.

He lifted his glass to his lips, then paused. "You okay? You look... worried."

She sucked in a long breath of the salty air. "I'm just a bit rusty on the whole dating thing.

Like a bazillion years rusty. And… I don't want things to change between us."

"So is that a no, now?" Disappointment slipped across his features.

"No, it's still a yes." She smiled weakly. "But… don't blame me if I mess this all up. You might regret asking me out. I might spill my drink, or trip, or bore you to tears."

"I doubt it." His lips twitched upward. "And if it makes you feel better, I don't date much either. Like only a few times in all the years I've been living here in Magnolia."

"Well, look at that. We're both a pair of amateurs."

"Guess we'll just have to figure it out together." He reached over and took her hand in his.

The warmth of his hand flowed through hers, giving her confidence that this new step in her life would work out okay. Maybe they'd just date a few times. Maybe only once. But she was willing to take this step with him. Try out this whole dating thing.

"I guess we *will* just figure it out together."

They sat there silently watching the sunset, her hand still firmly entwined with his. The peace of the moment wrapped around her like a beloved quilt, familiar, warm, secure. The sky broke into brilliant shades of oranges with slivers of purple scattered through them.

"A perfect sunset, isn't it?" Dale asked softly.

"It is. Perfect." Just like the moment.

CHAPTER 15

Maxine hummed as she went about her work on Friday, eagerly anticipating her date with Dale that evening, even if she was still nervous about it. Eleanor had just arrived, and Maxine was pouring her coffee when Darlene came in and headed right toward them.

"Knew I'd find you here, Eleanor."

Maxine's mouth dropped open in amazement. Just plain old Eleanor, not Miss Eleanor. That was interesting. She'd only seen Darlene a few times since checking out of the B&B and none of those times had hinted at the type of friendly relationship between Darlene and Eleanor that she was currently witnessing.

Darlene settled into the seat at the table, which also surprised Maxine. No one sat with

Miss Eleanor. Darlene leaned forward. "Did you hear that someone bought the two houses at the far end of the boardwalk? And the lots are side by side. Rumor has it that it's someone who wants to tear the houses down."

"I didn't hear that." Eleanor looked offended that Darlene had found out first. "You think they want to build a larger house there?"

"I'm not sure. But I also heard someone approached the council to get a variance to build higher than two stories."

"They wouldn't change that, would they?" Maxine asked.

Eleanor glared at her to let her know she was interrupting. "You never know with those fools sitting on the council these days."

"I miss having you on the council, Eleanor. You were always so levelheaded," Darlene said. "I knew the bridge would bring changes, but I'd hoped they'd be small ones. Still leave Magnolia Key feeling like... well, feeling like Magnolia Key. If one area gets a variance, what's stopping some high-rise modern condos or hotels? It would change everything."

"I'll be going to that meeting to stop this nonsense. Those ordinances were put in place for a reason. To protect the island. Protect the island's history. And I'm not a fan of people coming in and tearing down the older homes for new fancy, modern ones either." Eleanor scowled.

Maxine hurried away to the kitchen to get Miss Eleanor's muffin. "Hey, Beverly." She walked over to where Beverly was unloading the dishwasher. "Darlene just came in and she's sitting at Miss Eleanor's table. Not sure if that surprised me more or the fact that Darlene called Miss Eleanor, Eleanor."

Beverly laughed. "She's the only person in town that I know who calls her that."

"And Darlene said there's rumors going around that someone bought the two houses and lots at the end of the boardwalk. They're asking for a variance from the town council. Possibly to put up higher buildings."

Beverly frowned. "I hope that never happens. I guess I'll have to find out when the meeting is and be sure I go to it."

"That's what Miss Eleanor said. I'm not a registered voter here, so I guess I can't really offer up my opinion." Just another reminder she was still an outsider here. But then, she hadn't totally made up her mind if she was going to make Magnolia Key her permanent residence, so she hadn't changed her voter registration.

Beverly set a heated muffin on a plate and handed it to her. "It's hard to stop progress, and I don't mind some changes, but I would really hate to see big, tall buildings on the island."

"Miss Eleanor said the people on the town council were fools."

Beverly laughed. "She's not that far off. The group we have now is pretty set on passing things that help themselves rather than benefit the town. I'm hoping in the next election that we can get some new members on the council."

"Do you think that will be too late?"

"I hope not."

Maxine headed back out to bring Miss Eleanor her muffin, wondering if the town she'd come back home to was going to change before she even got used to being here again.

The morning got busy and Maxine didn't even see Eleanor and Darlene leave. But Eleanor left her payment for breakfast on the table. Since she got almost the same thing every time she came in, she didn't really need to see the bill.

She looked up as the door swept open, and Dale stood in the doorway. A little flutter jittered in her chest, which she ignored. She waved and gave him a just-a-minute sign while she finished taking the order of a group of ladies who came in on Fridays midmorning and played bridge with their coffee. She was getting to know the routines of the regulars.

She poured their coffee and turned in an order for a plate of cinnamon rolls, then hurried over to Dale. "Morning. Coming in for a late breakfast?"

"Ah, no." He shifted from foot to foot. "Uh, I already ate."

"Okay..." She stared at him.

"I just wanted to be sure you haven't changed your mind. That you're still going out with me tonight." He looked at her expectantly.

She laughed. "Yes, we're still going out. But I have to admit, I'm a bit nervous."

"Don't be. It's just... me. Pretend it's just like some other time we went to grab something to eat."

"Only it doesn't feel like that, does it?"

He shook his head. "No, it doesn't. It feels... special."

Special. He thought going out with her felt special...

"I'll let you get back to work. Just wanted to check." Relief spread across his face. "So we're still on."

"Still on."

"I'll pick you up at six."

"You're going to walk *all the way across the courtyard* to get me?" She pressed a hand to her heart and feigned shock.

"All the way. I'm a proper gentleman, you know." His eyes sparkled.

"I'll see you at six, then."

He left the cafe, and she turned to find Beverly grinning at her. "You two are cute together."

"What are you talking about?" She ducked her head and started clearing a table.

"Bet you have a great time on your date tonight."

"I hope so." She settled the tub of dishes against her hip. "I hope I don't do something silly, or wrong, or... something. I can't believe I'm going on a date."

"You'll be fine. You know, if you survive your nervousness and make it all the way until six." Beverly gave her a quick side hug and turned and headed away, shaking her head.

Beverly was probably right. They'd have a good time tonight and all this nervousness would be for nothing. Right?

CHAPTER 16

Dale stood in front of the mirror hanging over his dresser, adjusting the unruly collar of his blue button-down shirt. His aunt used to say this shirt brought out the color of his eyes. Did it? He stared at his reflection for a moment, undecided. Then he frowned, wondering if he should wear something more casual than this shirt. He could roll up the sleeves. That would give it a more casual look. He unbuttoned the cuffs and flipped up the sleeves, carefully rolling them up a couple of times. There, that looked better. Didn't it? Or did it?

"It's just dinner at Magic Cafe, not some kind of formal gala like the one over in Moonbeam when The Cabot Hotel had its grand opening. Get over yourself." He shook his head as he left the bedroom, glancing at his watch. Still too early to head over to Maxine's.

He picked up his wallet and keys and paced the floor, watching the minutes tick away on the clock. Nervousness swelled through him. The evening loomed ahead with a definite feeling of severe importance. The next step in his relationship with Maxine. A make-it-or-break-it night.

He admitted he had to caution himself around her, always afraid he was going to step on her toes. She so desperately wanted to make it on her own, fiercely guarding her independence. He got that. He did. He just didn't want to make a misstep. Especially when their relationship was so new.

Could he overthink this evening any more? The question hung in the empty room.

He grabbed the bouquet of flowers he'd gotten for Maxine and questioned that decision, too. It was a simple bouquet, nothing elegant or fancy, but their bright colors had caught his attention when he'd seen them in the window of the general store.

He stepped outside and took a deep breath, looking across the courtyard to Maxine's door.

He counted his steps as he crossed the distance. One. Two. Three…

"For Pete's sake. Get over yourself," he scolded himself under his breath. "It's just a date."

But tonight was different. A date. A subtle shift in their relationship. That must be why he felt so nervous. He climbed the steps to the guest house and heard the sound of music coming from inside. It sounded like classical music. Huh. That was something he didn't know about her. Her taste in music. How much did he really know about her, anyway? But wasn't this date a step in the direction of getting to know her better?

Grasping the flowers tightly, he lifted his hand and knocked, the sound much louder than he intended. He shifted back, anticipating her opening the door…

Maxine startled at the sound of the knock. Was it six already? She finished closing the clasp on her necklace and took one last look in the mirror. At her—what was it—third change of clothes?

Shaking her head at her indecision, she crossed to the door and opened it. Dale stood in the doorway, his hair still damp from a shower, wearing a crisp blue shirt that brought out the blue of his eyes. Did guys ever notice stuff like that?

"Hi, I brought you these." He thrust a bouquet of colorful flowers toward her.

"Thank you, they're beautiful. Come inside while I put them in a vase."

He followed her over to the kitchen, and she found a mason jar and filled it with water. She carefully arranged the blooms—were her hands shaking?—and set the jar on the table. "There, that looks nice." She pulled her hands back and twisted the bracelet on her wrist. Twice.

"It does." He nodded.

"They're pretty." So much small talk, but she couldn't quite mask the nervousness in her voice.

"I was hoping you'd like them. I wasn't sure if guys still brought things like flowers when they picked a woman up for a date. I guess it's old-fashioned." His eyes darted over to the arrangement, then back to her.

"I love them. It was very thoughtful."

Tension crackled between them in the ensuing silence.

"I guess—"

"We should probably—"

They both laughed. "You go first," Dale said.

"I was just saying we should probably go."

"You ready for our big adventure to Magic Cafe?"

"Adventure. I like that word better than... date." She laughed sheepishly. "I've worked myself up into quite a state worrying about this date with you. It's been a really long time since I've been on one."

"I've done a good job of talking myself into a bit of anxiety myself. So then, we'll think of this as an adventure, not a date." He winked, clearing away some of the tension.

"I guess we'll be nervous together." She smiled in response to his wink.

Knowing he was nervous, too, helped lighten her own unease. They headed out to his car, and he drove them to the ferry. When they reached the mainland, they headed to Belle Island.

They pulled into the crushed shell parking lot at Magic Cafe and he came around and opened the door for her. They walked inside and a she couldn't help but smile. "Oh, it looks the same. Just like I remember it."

"Hello, welcome to Magic Cafe," an older woman greeted them. "I'm Tally."

"Hi, Tally. Table for two," Dale said.

"I overheard your remark. So you've been here before?" Tally asked, her warm eyes sparkling with friendliness.

"I have, but I was just a girl the last time I was here. I've been away for... well, for a long time."

"You from around here?" Tally seated them at a table by the edge of the beach.

"He's from Magnolia Key," Maxine said. "Well, I guess I am, too. At least for now."

Dale seemed to hesitate for a moment before sitting down across from her.

"I'll send your server over right away. And I'm glad you decided to come back again. Always love to see repeat customers." Tally hurried away.

Dale set his menu down on the table. "So you're still thinking of leaving Magnolia? I thought that maybe... maybe you'd decided to stay."

"I haven't made any permanent decision.

I'm just kind of taking it day by day. Week by week." Though, she had to admit she had been toying with the idea of making Magnolia her home again. Change her address to here. Become a Florida resident again. She didn't know why it felt like such a huge step. And once she did make the decision, then... well, it was a huge change.

"Okay, sure. No pressure." But there was a bit of disappointment in his eyes mixed with understanding.

And she needed that now. Understanding. And someone willing to take things slowly. Because her life had spiraled out of control the last few years, and the last thing she needed was to make rash decisions.

Their meal was perfect, and Tally brought them complimentary slices of key lime pie at the end.

"Anyone who comes all the way from Magnolia Key to Magic Cafe deserves some dessert." Tally smiled. "Though, I guess once the bridge is finished, it will be a lot quicker to come here, won't it?"

"It will." Maxine took a spoonful of the pie, the tartness delighting her tastebuds. "This is so good."

Dale took a bite of his. "It is. I love key lime pie."

"Glad you like it," Tally said as she turned to leave.

Maxine took another bite, savoring the flavor. "Oh, I forgot to tell you. Did you hear that someone bought the last two houses at the end of the boardwalk?"

"No, I didn't." He frowned. "Both of them?"

"Darlene was in and said someone was asking for a variance on that property. To build to a higher height."

"That's not good. It will ruin the whole feel of the boardwalk if a high-rise looms over it."

"Beverly and Eleanor are planning to go to the city council meeting and speak against allowing the building height rules to be overturned."

"I'll make a point to go, too."

After dessert, they went out onto the beach and walked down to the water's edge.

"It's so pretty here," she said. "The turquoise water, the white sand."

"Pretty much what we have on Magnolia Key, isn't it?" he teased her.

"Yes. We're pretty lucky to live in this little

corner of the world, aren't we?" *We?* Maybe she was warming up to the idea of staying.

They headed back to the mainland and caught the last ferry back to Magnolia Key. He drove them home and walked her back to the guest house.

"I had a really wonderful time." Should she ask him in? Or maybe it was getting kind of late for that. She did have an early shift in the morning.

"I did too. We'll have to do it again soon. Go on an adventure, I mean." He grinned conspiratorially.

"Much better than a date." She nodded soberly, trying to hide her own grin that wanted to break free.

They stood there for a moment, hesitation swelling between them. Just as she shoved her hand out for a shake, he went in for a hug. They both laughed. He hugged her lightly and stepped back. "Sleep well."

He crossed the courtyard, and she waited until he disappeared inside and the lights turned on in his cottage before she stepped inside her own. She leaned back against the door.

For a moment, she'd been sure he was going

to kiss her. But no, just the awkward shake-hug dance they'd done.

But she wasn't ready for a kiss yet, anyway. Was she?

Oh, good. Overthinking everything again.

CHAPTER 17

Beverly hurried around getting ready for work the next morning. The house was so quiet in the mornings now without Maxine here. She was glad that Maxine was finding her footing back here in Magnolia. And happy that Maxine and Dale had become friends. And now had a date. Everything was falling into place for her friend.

It must have been kind of scary to have a date after all those years. She hadn't had one herself in… she didn't know how long. Well, that was a lie. She knew exactly the last man she'd dated. And look how that had turned out. But she didn't think about that—think about him—anymore, she reminded herself.

She drove to the ferry landing and arrived

just as the boat was pulling in. After getting her delivery of baked goods, she headed to Coastal Coffee. "Morning, Sal." She greeted the cook as she set the boxes on the counter.

"Morning." Sal nodded as he finished making the coffee.

"I peeked. There's strawberry muffins today."

"Nash will be happy about that."

Beverly headed out to write the day's specials on the chalkboard, then unlocked the door and flipped the sign to open. She was anxious for Maxine to come in so she could hear about her date.

Maxine arrived soon after that, a smile on her face.

"So you had a good time last night, huh?"

"I did." Her smile broadened. "Really nice."

"So you got over all your nervousness?"

"I did. You know, he said he was nervous, too." She laughed. "And somehow that made it all better."

"How was Magic Cafe?"

"Wonderful. Just like I remembered it."

"I haven't been there in over a year now, I think. Darlene and I went together last time. I should plan to go again soon."

"You should. The food is so good."

The cafe was soon busy, and they didn't have much time to chat. As the crowd died down, Beverly cornered Maxine for more questions. "So, tell me everything. Did he ask you out for another date?"

"He just said we'd do it again soon."

"That counts." Beverly bobbed her head. "Was it strange going on a date after all these years of not dating?"

"It was. Really strange. But it was also fun and a bit... I don't know... exhilarating? I never thought I'd be dating again after I married Victor. And then after he left, I was pretty anti-men. All men. And anyone who wanted any control over me." Maxine shrugged. "But now? It just seemed like the right time to take the first step."

"Dale's a good guy. Who better to go on a first date with?"

Maxine frowned. "How about you? When's the last time you went out on a date?"

"It's been awhile." She dodged any specifics.

"You should try it. It's kind of fun." Maxine grinned. "And... I'm kind of thinking of making this move to Magnolia permanent."

"You are? That's fabulous." Beverly hugged

her friend. "I love having you here. Not to mention you're a great employee." She laughed.

"I like it here, too. And I've missed you while I've been gone. I forgot how nice it is to have a friend like you to talk to. Most of my so-called friends back in Philadelphia were just parents I knew because of the kids."

The thought of having Maxine back permanently thrilled Beverly. She had a lot of friends here on Magnolia Key, but none of them were as close as she and Maxine had been. And they were becoming that close again.

"I love having my own place now. Decorating it just how I want. I'm having such fun with it."

Maxine sure was embracing her newfound independence. And her new home. A pang of—something—flittered through Beverly. She was happy for her friend. But in a way, it just made her same-same life seem predictable and a bit lonely. Going home alone each night to the empty cottage. Eating alone. Sitting out on her deck alone. Since when did that make her feel lonely?

She knew why, if she'd admit it to herself. Maxine's date had stirred up long-buried memories. Ones better left unthought of.

"Anyway, I'm not sure where this thing with Dale is going. Or if it's even a thing."

"But you should keep going and figure out where it's headed."

"I will… It's just kind of scary to think about getting involved with someone again. Victor leaving me was such a surprise. I had no clue. I feel foolish that I didn't see any of the signs."

"No one expects someone to just up and leave like that." No one. Not Maxine. Not… her.

"That's in the past." Maxine waved to a customer coming in the door. "And that's where it will stay." She headed over to greet the customer.

Sometimes keeping the past in the past was harder than you'd think. But she didn't have the nerve or energy or whatever to really confront her own past. And she didn't know if Maxine's courage in dating again gave her hope for herself that someday she'd try the whole dating thing again, or not.

Yes, sometimes keeping the past firmly buried did seem like the best way to handle it. She bustled away to take an order, leaving all thoughts of the past behind her. Mostly.

CHAPTER 18

A few evenings later, Dale had yet to say anything else about them going on an official date again, even though she'd seen him out on the beach the other morning. So she took the lead and asked him over for happy hour at her cottage tonight. There was a bottle of nice red wine open to breathe on the counter, and she'd made an appetizer that she found the recipe for online. Baked brie with apricot sauce all put in a puff pastry. She'd just pop it in the oven for them when it was time. She loved trying new recipes. Although things had changed since the days she would put together a big business dinner without much notice. She loved to cook, but it wasn't as much fun cooking for one. This was a nice reason to try something new.

The fairy lights she'd recently hung over the arched doorways in the main room created a festive but homey atmosphere. She'd always loved lights like this and had once made a lantern filled with ornaments, twine balls, and fairy lights for the corner of the living room. She'd thought it looked lovely. Victor had hated it and made her get rid of it. Maybe she'd make another one for here at her cottage. The freedom of making her own choices exhilarated her, and she hummed as she straightened the room and waited for Dale.

She answered his knock a few minutes later and couldn't help the immediate smile that popped on her face when she saw him. She grabbed his hand. "Here, come in."

He stepped inside. "Hope I'm not late. Got tied up at the shop."

"You're fine. Let me put the appetizer in the oven and we'll get our wine."

He followed her over to the kitchen. "I like these lights you put up. They add a warm glow to the room."

She blushed with pleasure at his compliment. "Thank you."

After she slipped the appetizer into the oven and set an alarm, they went over and settled on the couch.

"I see you finished your coffee table. It looks great." Dale reached for a coaster to set his drink on.

"I do think the cottage is coming together like I pictured it in my mind." Happiness swelled through her. Her life was finally settling down. Better than she'd imagined it ever would.

"What are you thinking about? You're smiling."

"I was just…" She shrugged. "I was thinking how happy I am here in Magnolia. And… I think I want to stay."

"You do?" A broad grin swept across his face. "That's great. Wonderful."

She matched his grin with one of her own. "I do. I'm just… happy here."

"I'm pretty happy myself these days." He reached out and took her hand. "I hope this means we can keep seeing each other. I wanted to ask you out on a date again but didn't want to rush you. And… to be honest… if you were just going to leave Magnolia Key, then it seemed a bit foolish to see where all this was going between us. Didn't want to get my heart stomped on." He threw her a rueful grin.

His heart was involved in all this? Did he have feelings for her?

He stood up and reached down a hand, pulling her to her feet. "And there's something I've been wanting to do. I mean, if it's okay with you. I've been wanting to kiss you."

"You have?" Her heart raced double time.

"I have. Do you think this might be a good time for our first kiss?" His eyes glittered with anticipation.

"I think this might be the perfect time." She held her breath as he leaned closer, feeling the soft brush of his fingers as he swept her hair back.

A loud knock rang through the cottage. Almost a pounding.

She stepped back, trying to catch her breath as her heart pounded in her chest. "I should get that."

He nodded as she hurried past him to answer the door. Someone had extremely lousy timing.

She gasped as she opened the door. "Tiffany, what are you doing here?" She glanced guiltily back at Dale like some schoolgirl caught kissing a boy. Or almost kissing.

"I came looking for you. We need—" Tiffany stopped short and stared at Dale. "Oh, hello."

Dale stepped forward and held out a hand. "Hi, I'm Dale."

"He's my landlord." It was the first thing that popped into her startled brain. "He, uh, lives next door. I rent this guesthouse from him." Her words rushed out.

"I see." Tiffany looked at Dale and back to her.

"Uh, well, I should go. Let you two catch up." Dale glanced at her briefly. He *almost* covered the look of disappointment in his eyes. "Nice to meet you, Tiffany."

She walked him to the door and took a step outside. "We'll talk later?"

"We will." His hand brushed hers briefly, and he smiled. "Soon."

She walked back inside. Tiffany stared at her for a moment, then shook her head. She half-expected her daughter to roll her eyes.

"We're just friends." As if she needed to

explain anything to her daughter. And calling Dale a friend wasn't quite the whole truth. "So, you were saying why you came to Magnolia?"

"Friends, huh?"

Tiffany looked like she didn't believe her. Or maybe looked like she didn't care one way or the other.

"You know, it's such a pain to get here. Flew into Sarasota, then took an Uber to the ferry. Then that horrible, sloshy ride across the bay. Then I couldn't find an Uber here."

"We don't have them here on the island. But I'm not a far walk from the landing." She frowned. "How did you find where I'm living?"

"Went to that Coastal Coffee, but they were already closed. Who closes so early? Anyway, Beverly saw me peeking in the window. She hasn't changed much, has she? And I haven't seen her in probably fifteen or twenty years when you used to drag us here for those boring visits. Anyway, she told me where you live."

"So you just came to check on me?" And why hadn't she called first?

"When are you coming home?" Tiffany set down a large tote bag and stood with her hands on her hips, demanding an answer. "You've been away long enough."

"I'm not sure… when I'm leaving." Or *if* she was leaving. But did she really want to have that argument with Tiffany now?

"Mom, we need you back home."

Now that shocked her. Her kids hadn't really needed her for anything since they learned to drive and Victor bought them both their own cars so she was no longer their chauffeur. "You need me back home?"

"Don't be silly. Of course we do."

Did they? Had she deserted them? Did they really need her? Want her back home? But the thing was, Magnolia Key was starting to feel like home to her. But if they needed her, how could she say no? She was their mother, after all.

"So, you'll come home?"

"I don't know…"

"I have some news for you. Maybe it will help you change your mind. I'm pregnant." Tiffany threw her arm out triumphantly.

"Oh, Tiff, that's great." She rushed to hug her daughter. Tiffany accepted the hug for a moment, then stepped back.

"So this changes everything, doesn't it?"

"I… I guess so?" Did it? She didn't want to miss being there when the baby was born. But she could go visit then. And visit lots. But did she really want to go and slip back into her old life there? Besides... she had no job there. No way to support herself.

"Good. So when are you coming home?"

"I didn't say I was for sure."

"You wouldn't come home for your grandchild?" Tiffany looked at her in disbelief.

"I've made a life for myself here. And like it here. I have a job." She was excited about the baby, but things had just started to fall into place for her now. All that would change if she moved back to Philadelphia.

"I bet Dad could find you a job with his company. Or maybe doing his business dinners. That woman he's seeing wouldn't know how to throw a dinner party if her life depended on it."

"No, that wouldn't work." Not at all. The last thing she needed to be was back under Victor's control. "How long are you staying? We'll talk more later."

"I was hoping for just one night."

"I'll give you my room. I'll take the couch."

"No, I booked a room at Bayside Bed and Breakfast. I hope it's nice."

"Oh, Darlene's B&B is lovely."

The oven timer went off. "Oh, I made an appetizer. Would you like some?"

"No, I'm beat. And I ate early over on the mainland. Wasn't sure if there were any nice places to eat here. All I could remember was burgers and fried food when we came here before."

Because that's what the kids had wanted to eat back then. She went and pulled the appetizer out of the oven and set it on the stovetop, looking at it longingly. It had browned perfectly and smelled heavenly.

"So, you'll drive me to the B&B?"

"Let me get my keys."

She drove Tiffany to Darlene's and walked her in. "Darlene, this is my daughter, Tiffany. She made a reservation."

"Oh, I didn't know she was your daughter." Darlene smiled warmly at Tiffany.

Tiffany didn't smile, just answered with, "Is my room ready?"

"It is." Darlene handed her a key. "First room on the right when you go upstairs."

"Does it have a view?"

"It does."

"Well, it will have to do. There's not a lot to choose from here on Magnolia Key."

"Tiffany!" She frowned at her daughter.

"What?" Tiffany shrugged. "There isn't."

"Do you want me to take your tote bag up for you?" Maxine offered, after giving Darlene an apologetic look.

"I've got it, Mom. I'm pregnant, not incapable." Her daughter rolled her eyes.

Ah, there was the look she remembered so well. She pasted on a smile, ignoring Tiffany's attitude.

"I'll see you tomorrow then. I'm working at Coastal Coffee in the morning. Maybe we could have lunch after that?"

"Fine. I'll meet you there about noon. But then I want to catch the ferry. I have an early evening flight out of Sarasota, and it takes forever to get to the airport from here."

"Okay, I'll see you tomorrow."

Tiffany headed up the stairs. She turned to Darlene. "She's tired." As if that excused her daughter.

"Pregnancy can really zap it out of you, can't it?"

"It can." But she wasn't sure that pregnancy made someone rude... She just hoped Tiffany was nice to Darlene when she came down for breakfast. "I should go. Good to see you."

Maxine headed out to her car and drove the few minutes it took to get back to her cottage.

She went inside and looked at the lovely appetizer she'd made. With renewed resolve, she popped it back in the oven to heat it up. She might as well enjoy it.

She sat with her brie and wine, mulling over Tiffany's visit. She was extremely happy for Tiffany and the pregnancy. She had really thought her daughter would never have children. She never seemed interested in them. But maybe her husband had wanted them. She wouldn't know. She wasn't close to Tiffany's husband at all. He was kind of a standoffish guy.

But now she did have some hard decisions to make. Why had this happened right after she'd decided to make Magnolia Key her home?

And to be honest, Tiffany's attitude annoyed her. She'd forgotten how thoughtless Tiffany could be.

But how could she stay here when her first grandchild was being born? And Tiffany said she needed her. She was probably overwhelmed with the thought of having a baby. Babies could be scary. She remembered when she brought David home. She couldn't believe those nurses just let her take this human being home with her. That she was responsible for him. What did she know about babies? But, like every mother, she'd learned.

And she'd loved being a mother. Especially when the kids were young. Back when... they liked her.

How could she go back to Philadelphia and put up with Tiffany's attitude? The eye rolling. Always being treated like she didn't know anything, or did things wrong. But surely that would change when the baby was born. Because she'd know how to take care of it.

She wondered if Tiffany knew if it was a boy or a girl. She hadn't said.

Why did life keep throwing her curves?

CHAPTER 19

The next morning, Beverly looked up to see Maxine rushing into Coastal Coffee. "I'm sorry. I tossed and turned all night. Hit the snooze on my alarm. I'm really sorry."

"We just opened. It's fine." Beverly frowned, concerned about her friend. It wasn't like Maxine to be late for work. "You do look tired, though. You okay?"

"I'm… no, I'm not."

"My guess is it has to do with Tiffany's arrival."

"It does. She wants me to move back to Philadelphia."

"But did you tell her you'd decided to stay here?"

"No… because…" Maxine let out a long

sigh. "Because she said she needed me home. And... she told me she's pregnant."

"She is? Well, congrats, Grandma. That's great news." She hugged her friend, then stepped back and frowned again. "So why don't you seem happier?"

"I am happy about the baby. A grandchild. I never thought it would happen."

"But it throws a wrench into you wanting to live here?" She could see how torn Maxine was.

"I do want to live here. I have a job, a home. I'm just getting settled. Back in Philadelphia I have no job. No place to live."

"They've made this invention called the airplane," she teased. "You could always go back and visit as much as you wanted."

"But... she said she needed me." Maxine shook her head. "And there's more."

"Tell me."

"She was just so... dismissive of me. Kind of like how Victor used to be with me. I don't know if I can go back and be treated like that."

"Then stay here. Go there when the baby is born and help out, then come back." That seemed like the logical approach to Beverly. Why should Maxine go back and subject herself to not being treated like she deserved to be?

"I don't know. It's been a long time since I've heard one of my kids say they needed me. I just don't know what to do. It's been so rocky with the kids and me. But maybe this would be a great second chance. A new stage of life for us."

"This is one decision you're going to have to make on your own. I'll support you with anything you decide. But I'll sure miss you if you leave. I've gotten used to having you around again."

Maxine's face clouded. "And I just told Dale last night that I'd decided to stay."

"You did?"

"He was happy. And he… he started to kiss me. But then Tiffany's arrival interrupted us."

"You do have a lot to weigh with this decision, don't you?" Beverly hugged her again. "But take your time. Don't rush into anything. You'll figure out what's best."

"Will I?" Maxine shook her head and headed into the kitchen.

Beverly didn't envy her. It would be a difficult decision to make. Beverly had never been overly fond of Maxine's children. They always acted like they were better than the people on Magnolia Key. And she didn't like the way they talked to Maxine, either. But they were

Maxine's kids, and she knew Maxine loved them.

Maxine went about her job that morning, smiling at customers, but she didn't fool Beverly. She could tell she was upset. But she never let it affect her job. Where was she ever going to find someone to replace Maxine at Coastal Coffee if she left? She immediately felt selfish for the thought. Maxine had to do what was best for her.

Tiffany and Darlene came in about noon. "Is Mom here?" Tiffany swept her gaze around the shop, which evidently didn't meet with her approval as a look of disparagement settled on her face.

Beverly plastered on a wide smile, ignoring Tiffany's look. Well, pretty much ignoring it. "She's in back. I'll tell her you're here. Darlene, you here for lunch?"

"No, I just drove Tiffany over here. She didn't feel like walking."

"I see. Tiffany, why don't you just grab a table and I'll get your mom."

Tiffany nodded, and with no thank you to Darlene, headed over to a table.

"I should get back. My knitting group is

meeting at the B&B this afternoon. We'll talk later."

"Thanks for bringing Tiffany over."

"No problem." Darlene hurried out.

Beverly headed to the kitchen. "Your daughter is here. Darlene drove her over."

"Oh, I should have gone to pick her up."

"It's a five-minute walk, tops." All Tiffany had was a good-sized tote for her overnight bag.

"She's… tired with the pregnancy."

Beverly just nodded as Maxine headed out to find Tiffany. More like Tiffany was self-centered and spoiled. But she was also Maxine's kid, so she kept her thoughts to herself.

Maxine hurried out to Tiffany and sat across the table from her. "Are you hungry? Or would you like some tea or something?"

"No, nothing from here." Her daughter wrinkled her nose.

Maxine silently counted to ten, unwilling to call her out on her snobbish remark. At least her daughter had come here to Magnolia to see her. She focused on that.

"I'll get something in Sarasota. I want to catch the next ferry. But I wanted to talk to you and see when you're coming home. Soon, right?"

"I'm not sure." All these thoughts whirled around in her mind. She needed some time to herself to figure it all out.

"What's not to be sure about? David and I need you back home."

They hadn't needed her for years, but maybe Tiffany did need her now. Just needed the reassurance her mother was near if she needed her. How could she be so selfish as to consider staying here when Tiffany needed her? What kind of mother would she be?

"I have to consider everything. My job. The life I've made here."

"What about me? The baby? Aren't you going to consider us?"

"Of course, sweetie, I just have a lot to think about." But why was she even considering not moving back? Tiffany needed her. That should be enough. "I don't have a job there. A place to live."

"You could live in the apartment over our garage until you find a place."

That would solve one problem. She'd seen it once, and it was a cramped, tiny space. Better suited for a small office, which was what Tiffany's husband used it for. But it would work, she guessed.

"I'll think about it, honey. Really, I will."

Tiffany rose from the table and grabbed her tote. "I never thought of you as a self-centered person. I guess I was wrong."

"Tiff—" She stood up and reached for her daughter.

Her daughter held up a hand. "No, don't, Mom. You do what you have to do. You always do anyway, don't you?"

"What does that mean?" She'd done everything for her family. Everything.

"Dad told me how you just wouldn't do what he needed. Couldn't become the person he needed you to be. How he'd suggested a lady that would help you pick out clothes for his business functions. I mean, seriously, Mom. Sometimes you dress like... well, someone who doesn't know how to dress properly."

She looked down at her worn khaki pants and the Coastal Coffee t-shirt she had on. She'd always preferred comfortable clothes to fancy clothes. But she had picked out nice dresses to wear to Victor's many functions. Hadn't she? She did remember him giving her a card for some stylist, but she'd put the card in a drawer, thinking she didn't need one. But had she needed one? Insecurity swept through her.

"And how you were too busy to do the things he needed you to do. Run the errands he needed done."

Her mouth actually dropped open. "He said that?"

"You were just never willing to change, were you? To be what he needed, so our family could stay together. And now… you're only thinking of yourself. Not me. Not the baby. Not David. But I guess that's how you've always been."

She plunked back down in her chair, stunned. Victor had said this is why they'd divorced? Not that he'd been cheating on her? Was it really her fault that the family fell apart?

"You wouldn't even get a job." Her daughter looked at her with such disdain. Such contempt. Was this really how her children thought of her?

Not to mention that Victor had forbidden her to get a job. Even when she'd found one at the local bookstore that would work her hours around the kids' schedule. He wouldn't hear of it.

"What have you really done with your life? And now—" Tiffany swept her gaze around the cafe. "Now you're working in a coffee shop. It's embarrassing. What will I tell people if they ask what you do?"

"This is a perfectly respectable job. I love working here." She quickly defended the cafe.

"Whatever." Tiffany rolled her eyes. "I thought that maybe you'd come back and try to make things right. But I guess you always just think of yourself."

"I just need some time to decide. Surely you understand that."

"No, I don't understand what there is to decide. What is keeping you here?" Tiffany flicked her hair behind her shoulder. "But I guess you always just think of yourself. Think of what *you* want."

She had never in her life put herself before her family. Never put herself first with anything. Her heart clenched in her chest and she struggled against the tears.

"I have to go so I don't miss the ferry to start the ridiculously tortuous trip to get back home. Let me know when you decide." She spun around and strode out of the cafe. No hug. No goodbye.

Beverly walked up to her and sat down. "I

heard most of that. I'm sorry. Don't take what she said to heart. You're a wonderful mother."

"Am I? Was I?" A lone tear traveled down her cheek. "Maybe it was my fault. Maybe I wasn't willing to be what Victor needed. And now… Tiffany just looks at me with disgust."

"Maxine, you've been my best friend my whole life, so I say this with all the love I have for you. You need to learn to stand up for yourself." Beverly reached over and took her hand. "Your daughter is wrong. She's only thinking of what she wants. Not what you need. And for the record, you did everything for that family of yours. Everything. Don't let anyone tell you differently."

She dashed at the tear. "Thank you for that. And I know I should have stood up to her. I was just shocked at her anger toward me. She's probably right. I should go back home. Help her with the baby. See what I can salvage of our family."

"I think you should consider what it is *you* need now. It's okay, you know, to make the life you want for yourself. Your children are adults now. They have their own lives. You're allowed to have yours too." Beverly rose. "You okay?"

"I'm fine. Really, I am."

Beverly looked at her skeptically.

She sighed. It didn't sound convincing to her, either. "I will be fine. I just need time to sort it all out." She stood. "And keeping busy is just what I need." But somehow she wasn't sure she could ever stay busy enough to keep her thoughts from whirling around her brain.

CHAPTER 20

Maxine tossed and turned all night. Replaying her conversation with Tiffany. Replaying scenes from her marriage. Maybe Tiffany was right. Maybe she had refused to change and be the person Victor wanted her to be. But should she have had to change to please him? Shouldn't both people in a marriage give some? She'd done so much that he wanted. Spent her life making his life run smoothly. And let him decide she couldn't take a job she wanted to take. He always made the decisions about everything. Where they would live. How the house was decorated. Where they'd vacation—at places that would impress people when he talked about them—though she had to make all the detailed travel plans.

How had their marriage gotten to that point? Where she'd let him decide everything? She rolled over, punched the pillow, and settled back down. Still, sleep eluded her.

At five, she crawled out of bed and got dressed, still no closer to making a decision. She walked out to the beach with her coffee, hoping something would help her decide. Sinking down on the cool sand, she sipped a taste of the coffee and waited for the sky to lighten.

"I thought I saw you out here." Dale dropped to the sand beside her. "I thought you might come over last night. Was Tiffany still in town?"

The early morning light highlighted his still-damp hair. "Ah... no. Tiffany left early afternoon. I just needed some time."

He took her hand in his. "That's okay. We don't have to let anyone know about us yet. Not until we figure things out." He smiled at her. "But I'd sure like that kiss your daughter interrupted."

He started to lean closer, and she pulled back, holding up a hand. "Wait. I... I have to tell you something."

He bobbed his head. "Sure."

"See, the thing is… Tiffany wants me to move back to Philadelphia. She needs me now. She's… pregnant, and she wants me back there. She actually said she needed me." Along with a lot of other things, but no need to get into all that with Dale.

"Your first grandchild. That's something, isn't it?" He looked at her tentatively.

"It is. I'm happy for her. It's just… I like it here. My job. The guesthouse." And she almost said she liked him. But that wouldn't be fair, would it? Not if she was leaving.

"I see. So now you have to decide whether your decision to stay here in Magnolia is the right one, or whether you're headed back up east."

"Dale, I'm sorry. I know I said I was staying. But that was before I found out about Tiffany."

"I see. I guess this changes everything."

"I'm afraid it does. If I go back, I can help her. And… she said she needed me. That's hard to refuse. She hasn't needed me in a very long time." And she had to admit, it felt very nice to be needed.

"So you've decided? You're leaving?" Disappointment settled in his eyes.

"Don't be mad. I just think if she needs me, I have to go."

"I'm not mad." His voice was barely over a whisper. "I'm just sorry we won't have a chance to see where this was heading with us."

"I'm sorry too. About everything. I just feel like what kind of mother would I be if I don't go back when she needs me?"

"And what do *you* need?"

But she didn't answer him. Because what she needed wasn't important now. It was what her daughter needed.

Pain clouded his eyes and she could feel him distancing himself even as they sat there. A wall of cold, hard silence settled between them.

Finally, Dale stood. "I should go get ready for work." He started to walk back to his cottage and paused, turning back. "I should have known this was coming. That you'd leave."

She swallowed and tried to fight back the tears. "I'll miss you," she whispered as he walked away.

She guessed her decision had been made. She'd go back to Philadelphia where she was needed. And see if she could make things right with her children. Especially if they thought the family disintegrating was all her fault. Not that she'd tell them about Victor's infidelity. That wasn't something they needed to know. He was still their father.

She took a long, deep breath of the fresh sea air. She'd miss this. Miss so many things about Magnolia. She glanced at Dale's cottage. Miss so many people. One in particular.

Dale sat hunched inside his cottage, the warmth of his coffee mug providing little comfort. The walls closed in on him, trapping him, and he longed to sit outside on his deck. But he was afraid that Maxine might head back from the beach, and he didn't want to see her. He needed time. He'd just begun to believe that there was something between them. That they could have a relationship. And he'd let himself acknowledge he cared about her. Had feelings for her.

He set his mug down and it clinked against the wooden table, echoing around the cottage and highlighting the quiet of the empty room. He got up and paced the floor.

This was all his own fault. He knew better.

Had he not learned his lesson before? Women left him. There was always something more important than him in their lives. Something they chose over him.

He'd protected his heart for years after his last girlfriend broke up with him. And now, just when he was starting to trust Maxine—trust that it was okay to have feelings for her—then this happened. She was leaving. Leaving Magnolia. Leaving him.

He understood why she wanted to go. She felt she needed to be there for her daughter. He got that. There always seemed to be something more important than he was to any woman. His last girlfriend's job was more important. Maxine's family was more important.

He walked to the window but didn't see Maxine sitting out on the beach any longer. Which was good. Because he didn't want to see her. It was just too hard.

He wondered how long Maxine would stay in town. Hopefully, she'd leave soon, so he wouldn't keep running into her. Each day would just be ticking down the time until her inevitable departure.

The sooner she left, the sooner he could get

over her. In the meantime, he'd do everything possible to avoid her.

And the next time he felt even a flicker of interest in some woman, he'd squash it immediately. Not that there would be a next time. He was finished with women.

CHAPTER 21

Maxine worked on painting a changing table for one of the customers at Coastal Coffee who'd seen the bookcase and heard Judy rave about her coffee table. She needed to get this finished before leaving. And her plans to have a corner of Dale's shop with her refinished furniture? All that was scrapped now too.

She hadn't yet gotten up the nerve to call Tiffany and say she was moving back to Philadelphia. Because if she called and told her, the decision was final. Well, it already was kind of final. She'd told Beverly and Dale she was leaving. She knew she was just stalling. But the thought of leaving all she'd found here in Magnolia made her heart ache. This was the first time in years and years that she'd felt needed and like she had a chance to feel like she belonged.

And the thought of all the details of moving overwhelmed her. She'd have to ship her things back to Philadelphia. Not that they'd fit in the apartment over Tiffany's garage. They'd have to go back into storage. She wondered if she'd ever have a place again that she loved as much as this guesthouse. Surrounded by all her things. Decorated exactly like she wanted it.

And then there was Dale. She liked him. Liked him a lot. She'd seen him in the park this week, working on the repairs to the gazebo that Miss Eleanor had requested. When she stopped to say hi, the awkwardness between them was too much and she'd made an excuse to hurry off.

He hadn't come into Coastal Coffee even once over the last two weeks. Not once. But it shouldn't hurt her feelings because she was the one who was leaving. She was the one who had ended things between them... before they'd hardly even had a chance to start.

She stood up and stretched, her back aching from twisting around as she painted the changing table. She'd briefly thought about making a changing table for Tiffany and the baby, but then she wasn't sure her daughter would appreciate it. More than likely she'd go for some fancy, name-brand nursery set. She was like Victor in that way. Buying things she thought would impress people.

She worried about fitting back into a life back in Philadelphia. Worried about how Tiffany would treat her. But maybe when Tiffany saw how she was with the baby, she'd change her opinion and start to respect her more. When she found out just how much work a child was, maybe she'd realize how much her mother had put into raising both of her children.

A knock startled her, and she put her paintbrush down to go answer. Her mouth dropped open as she saw both her children standing in the doorway. "David, Tiffany, what are you doing here?"

David stepped inside. "Tiffany said she hadn't heard from you." Her son peered closely at her. "Mom, you have paint on your face."

She swiped at her face. "Oh, I was painting a changing table for a customer."

"So you're doing that to earn money too? See, Mom, this just isn't working out for you at all. You need to come back." Tiffany's tone left no room for argument.

And yet, she couldn't really tolerate being told what to do again. It was just like when she was married to Victor. No choices. Being told what she was doing and when she was doing it.

David shook his head disapprovingly. "Anyway, we came to convince you to come home." He looked at his watch. "I even took time off work to come here. Wasn't a good time to be away from work either."

It wasn't like she'd asked him to come...

"You should come back with us tomorrow. We'll arrange to have your things shipped." He glanced at his watch again.

"I couldn't leave tomorrow. I couldn't just leave Beverly shorthanded without a server. I need to give her notice. And wrap up loose ends here."

"So, you are planning on coming back?" Tiffany crossed her arms.

"I... I think so."

"Mom, I think so isn't an answer. Tiffany needs you. She told you that. What's to think about?"

"David, it's a big change for me."

Her son flicked his hand as if to swat away

her words as insignificant. "You can't want to stay here in this tiny place and wait tables. For Pete's sake, Mom. Be realistic. Enough of this silliness."

Anger swelled in her at his easy dismissal of her life here in Magnolia Key."I am being realistic. I have a job here. A place to live. I'd have to start all over in Philadelphia."

"You want to miss out on the birth of your grandchild?" Tiffany's eyebrows arched.

"No, I could fly back for that." Why was she delaying just telling them she'd go back?

David's phone rang, and he grabbed it from his pocket. He turned, walking out the door as he answered the call. "No, I'm sorry. Had to be out of the office. Will be back late tomorrow. I can meet with you then. How about dinner?"

He closed the door behind him, and she was left with Tiffany. "He's right, you know. This is no kind of life for you. On this tiny little island with nothing going for it."

"Magnolia Key has a lot going for it. It's a charming place and I love it here."

Tiffany looked slightly surprised that she'd contradicted her.

"Okay, I can see it might have some charm in an old-fashioned way. But there's no modern conveniences. You have to take a ferry to get to any normal grocery store or do any kind of shopping really. You have no family here. You don't belong here."

And that last sentence struck at her heart. Tiffany was right. She didn't really belong here. She wasn't one of them anymore. She'd tried, but just hadn't quite made it to the point where she was one of them again.

Or maybe she'd held herself back from feeling like she belonged. But it was too late because she was leaving, anyway.

David poked his head in. "I've got to make some more calls. You ready to head to the bed-and-breakfast, sis? Have you convinced Mom to come home?"

Tiffany tilted her head. "Have I?"

She took a deep, steadying breath. "Yes, I'll move back. I can't leave tomorrow like David suggested. But I will come back after I settle things here."

David nodded briskly. "Of course. Sensible decision. Come by the B&B in the morning and we'll make arrangements. We're leaving on the eleven o'clock ferry."

She didn't like how he just assumed she'd be there when he commanded. She was supposed to have the early shift at Coastal Coffee, but she'd talk to Beverly and see if she could leave early.

"I'll be there about ten."

"Let's go. I have work to do. This has already interrupted enough of my day." David turned and climbed down the front steps.

Tiffany followed behind him. "You made the right decision, Mom."

She just nodded as they drove away in their rental car. Had she made the right decision? But really, what choice did she have? Tiffany needed her. And she would always put her children first.

CHAPTER 22

Maxine threw herself into her job the next morning. Avoiding thinking about moving away. She'd told Beverly about the kids' visit and her final-final decision. She was for sure moving. She'd give Beverly time to find more help for the shop.

"Are you sure this is what you want to do?" Beverly asked. "You're certain?"

"I am. Tiffany needs me. It's scary thinking about being a first-time mom. And it's good to feel needed by her again."

"Then I'm glad for you. I'll miss you, but I'm happy for you. When are you leaving?"

"I guess in about a month. Will that give you time to find someone to work here?"

"Don't worry about me. I've been running

Coastal Coffee long enough. I'll find someone. Whoever I find will never replace you, though. I'll miss you."

"I'll miss you too."

Just then, Miss Eleanor came in and headed to her table.

"I've got her," Maxine said as she followed her across the room. "Good morning, Miss Eleanor."

Eleanor nodded and settled into her chair. She glanced at the chalkboard. "I'll have the lemon poppy seed muffin." She eyed Maxine. "And my coffee, of course."

"Of course." Maxine hurried to get the pitcher of cream and Miss Eleanor's coffee, then circled back around with the muffin. "Anything else?"

Miss Eleanor looked up at her. "I hear you're leaving the island."

She squirmed under the woman's gaze. "I... I am."

Miss Eleanor shook her head. "Not sure why. Seems like you have a pretty good thing going here. Job with Beverly. Home to stay in. And I heard you have a nice side business starting up with redoing furniture. It was good to see you start to stand on your own two feet."

She wasn't sure if that was a compliment or criticism.

"Aren't you going to miss all this?"

"I am," she replied honestly. "I'll miss it a lot. But I have responsibilities. I'm needed back home."

Eleanor eyed her for a long moment. "Sometimes when you do what other people want you to do, instead of what you want to do... well, it can have grave consequences. Your life might not turn out like you expected. How you wanted it to."

"I... know. But I have family obligations."

"Ah, family." Eleanor nodded. "They can sometimes make the heaviest demands of all."

CHAPTER 23

M axine hurried over to Darlene's, hoping she wasn't going to be late. She didn't want to see the disapproval in David's eyes if she was. Or see him glance at his watch over and over. Victor had always done the exact same thing. Looked at his watch as if you were bothering him and interrupting his day. David had perfected the same annoying habit.

Darlene was out sweeping the porch when she arrived and welcomed her with a warm smile. "Good morning, Maxine. Your kids are in the study drinking coffee. Go right on in."

"Thanks, Darlene." She hoped Tiffany hadn't been rude to Darlene this time.

She went inside, and the sound of Tiffany's

animated voice caught her attention. She paused inside the doorway.

"I knew if you came, we'd convince her to move back," Tiffany said with a self-satisfied tone in her voice.

"That solves your problem of finding a nanny, doesn't it? I'm sure she'll agree to watching your kid. Why wouldn't she? She has nothing else worth doing. It's not like she's going to wait tables back home."

"It will save us a lot of money if we don't have to pay for a nanny. And I want to get back to work as soon as possible after it's born. I wasn't ready for this surprise, but I want to make sure it changes my life as little as possible."

Maxine sagged against the door, listening in on their conversation, her heart pounding as anger swelled up inside her.

"And offering up the garage apartment was brilliant. She can even get up for those middle-of-the-night feedings," David added confidently.

"Yes, that's what I was thinking. We'll put in an intercom. And she'll be back in town and can take care of planning that big business dinner you want to have. That will impress your bosses. I admit, she is really good at organizing things like that."

"She is. And I plan to take full advantage of that. And I think I'll offer to head up the charity ball the company sponsors each year. My boss will like that. I'm so close to getting that promotion. This might seal the deal. Mom can figure all that charity stuff out for me."

"Things will finally get back to normal with her back and taking care of things."

Tiffany's smug tone made anger swell through her. Maxine swallowed hard, took a deep breath, and pushed off the wall. She strode into the sitting room.

"Mom, there you are." David looked at his watch, checking to see if she was on time. On *his* scheduled time.

She just barely kept herself from snatching the watch off his wrist. "Yes, I'm here. As you requested. No, as you told me to do."

David's forehead creased, and he set his coffee down on the side table, ignoring the stack of coasters. She walked across the room, grabbed one, and put his coffee cup on it.

She turned to face Tiffany, feeling the flush creep across her face as her anger rose up inside her. She clenched her jaw. "Do you plan on me watching your baby full time?"

"I… uh… I thought you might like to."

"Like to raise another child? Full time? After raising you two? And you just expected me to do this without even asking me?"

"I thought—"

Maxine held out her hand and cut her off. "Yes, that's the problem. You thought of what was best for you. Not what's best for that baby you're carrying. Only yourself."

She whirled around and faced David. "And you think that I'm going to spend my time taking care of your business affairs, too? You think that's how I want to spend my time?"

"Mom, were you eavesdropping?" His eyes flashed as he accused her.

"You bet I was. And I can't believe what I heard." She whirled back around to face Tiffany. "You said you needed me. You wanted me back home. But you just need someone to take care of that baby. But guess what? That baby is your responsibility and will be its whole life. No one else can take that over. Deciding to have a baby is a big responsibility."

"I didn't decide to. It was an accident," Tiffany shot back.

"And I hope that child never finds that out. I hope that child feels loved and wanted. You need to grow up, Tiffany."

Her daughter's eyes widened, and she gasped. "What did you say?"

"I said you need to grow up. You're an adult. It's time you acted like one instead of a spoiled brat. Part of that is my fault. I let you get away with a lot of things. Like your rudeness to people. The way you act like you're better than the people living on this island. Well, I'm here to tell you that you're not. These are good, hardworking people. They are here for each other. Respect each other." Her growing anger gave her strength to speak what she should have said years ago.

"Mom, I think you're getting a bit overwrought." David's patronizing tone was impossible to ignore.

"Don't talk to me like that," she snapped back at him. "I'm your mother. You should at least act like you respect me."

She stepped back and looked at both of them. "I'm so disappointed in both of you. In your attitudes. The way you put yourselves first. How did I raise such self-centered children? The way you think nothing of asking me to drop everything in the life I've worked so hard to build after your father left me... and come back to do your bidding."

"It's not like that." Tiffany's eyes glistened with the beginning of panic.

"It isn't going to be like that. Because I'm not moving back to Philadelphia." And a strong sense of peace, of rightness, soared through her at the words. "I'm staying here in Magnolia Key. I'll come visit the baby as often as I can. I'd like to be there for the birth if you'll let me. But I won't be moving back."

David stood up, shaking his head dismissively. "You'll come to your senses soon enough. You'll get tired of your life here. Then you'll come home. And when you finally do? Just see if we'll help you out then."

"I have come to my senses. That's why I'm staying."

"David, look what you've done. You've made her mad and now what am I going to do?" Tiffany jumped up and stood by her brother, poking a finger at his chest.

"What I did? I was just trying to get her to come back home. You failed last time."

"Stop it." Her words rang through the room as they both turned to stare at her.

"Go home. Figure out your lives. And while you're doing that, I'm going to live my own life."

She turned and strode out of the room, across the hall, and out the door. The sunshine and fresh air wrapped around her like a welcoming hug. A hug from Magnolia Key. Like the island agreed with her decision.

CHAPTER 24

Beverly looked up as Maxine rushed into the Coastal Coffee and grabbed her hand. "Beverly, come into the kitchen for a moment."

"Janine, hold down the fort. We'll be back out in a few minutes." Beverly let Maxine lead her to the kitchen.

"I'm staying." Maxine whirled around to face her.

A smile spread across her face. "You are? What made you change your mind?"

"Something Miss Eleanor said about doing what other people want you to do instead of what you need to do."

"Miss Eleanor made you change your mind?"

"Well, that and I overheard my kids talking.

They just wanted me back to take care of the details of their lives. Tiffany expected me to watch her baby full time. Without even asking me. And I heard her tell David I would be doing the middle-of-the-night feedings too. And David wants me to run some big charity thing to impress his boss. I just…" She held up her hands. "I can't go back to living like that. Doing what other people want me to do. Being under other people's control. I can't."

"So you told them all that?"

Maxine grinned. "All that and a lot more. I told them to grow up."

Well, that was a long time coming and much needed. "Good for you. I'm thrilled to have you staying here." She pulled her friend into a long hug. "I've gotten so used to you being here. Talking to you. And I think you did the right thing."

"I know I did. I looked at my kids, and I don't even know them. Not really. I love them, but I don't really like the people they've become." Maxine frowned. "I don't know if that's something I should admit."

"Hey, if it's the truth. And really, it was time to shove them out of the nest. Maybe they'll surprise you. Rise to the occasion."

"I hope so. For that baby's sake, if no one else's."

Janine poked her head in the door. "Dale's out here looking for you."

"Me?" Maxine said.

"Nope, Beverly."

"Let's go see what he wants." They walked back out into the shop. "Hi, Dale. What's up?"

He looked a bit taken aback to see Maxine standing here with her. "Oh, hi." He nodded at Maxine.

The three of them just stood there as she waited for Dale to explain why he wanted to see her.

"Oh, right. Why I came in." Dale pulled out a folder. "I did some digging and found out something interesting about the painting you found."

"What did you find out?"

"I found this old photo and I'm pretty sure it's the same location as in the painting." He pulled out a photo, and they peered at it.

"It sure looks like it." Beverly frowned. "It even has the walkway on top, like ours did. The widow's walk. Ours had been closed off for years before the building was even destroyed."

"And if you look closely, you can see this

carving over the door. Here, use this magnifying glass."

Beverly took the glass and looked closely at the photo. "It has the same carving that ours had. With the intertwined M and B."

"It does. And then I found out that Magnolia Key used to have a sister island. A small island off the country of Bardonzia. In the Pacific Ocean. About halfway between the United States and Australia. That was kind of a thing back then to have sister islands."

"I've never heard of this Bardonzia."

"Not surprised. It's a small country and quite a ways from here."

"So you think this painting is of Bardonzia?"

"I'm not sure, but I think so. My theory is that this painting is of their landing. I need to do more digging before I'm certain."

"But how do you think it ended up here? And why was it hidden?" Maxine said as she stepped forward.

Dale stepped back.

Beverly shook her head at them. They'd have to sort all this out themselves after Maxine told him she was staying.

"Anyway, I'll keep trying to find out more

information. I do love working on this little town mystery."

"I can't believe how much you've already figured out. Maybe I'll put the word Bardonzia up near the painting and see if anyone knows more about it. Someone should if they really were our sister island."

"That's a good idea." Dale took back the photo. "I should go now." He turned and hurried out the door.

Beverly turned to Maxine. "You need to talk to him, you know. Tell him you're staying."

"I know. But… I told him I was leaving. And I know that's a big thing with him. Just as he started to trust me, I decided to leave. I don't think he'll take a chance on me again."

"But you won't know until you talk to him, will you?"

"I'll try to talk to him tonight. You know, if he'll listen to me."

Dale hurried out of Coastal Coffee. Of course, he'd known there was a chance of seeing Maxine if he went into Beverly's shop, but he'd been so excited to share his news. But seeing Maxine still here tore at his heart.

He knew she was still in town. There had been no sign of her moving out yet. But he'd done his best to avoid seeing her. He stayed in his cottage when he was at home, no longer going out on the beach. He didn't even sit out on his deck, just in case she'd walk by on her way to or from the beach. The courtyard was off limits too.

He spent long hours working at Second Finds and came home late each night. He rearranged the shop and filled the corner where he'd planned to add the coastal furniture that Maxine was going to provide. All those plans were gone now.

And he felt like a horrible person for being so angry with her because he really did understand why she was going back to Philadelphia. She was a good person and wanted to take care of her daughter. He got that. But it didn't make it any easier to accept.

His heart clenched, and he realized he was still standing outside the door to Coastal Coffee, lost in his thoughts. He spun around and headed back to his shop, putting as much distance between him and Maxine as possible. As if that would fix his heart.

He'd spent every minute since she'd told him she was leaving trying to convince himself he had no feelings for her. And he was almost starting to believe it. Except... when he'd seen her, he knew he was just a big fat liar. The feelings were still there.

But maybe he could keep those feelings as a reminder to never let his guard down again. That's what any sane person would do. And never let themself be put in a position to get hurt again.

CHAPTER 25

Maxine kept looking out the window of the guest house, watching for Dale to come home. The last week or so he'd been coming home later and later. Avoiding her, of course. She didn't blame him. But now she needed to talk to him. Explain how her plans had changed. And maybe he'd give them another chance.

She walked over to the window and saw a light on in his cottage. Finally. She marched over, surrounding herself with as much courage as possible, and knocked on his door. When he didn't answer, she knocked again. Louder.

Finally, the door swung open, and he stood, looking… well… looking good. Handsome. And annoyed.

"Yes?" He didn't ask her in.

"I wondered if we could talk."

"I'm not sure there's anything else to say. I understand why you need to leave. I do. But I'd rather we not see each other while you're still here." He ran his fingers through his hair as he quickly hid the hint of pain that flitted through his eyes. "Honestly? It's just too hard to see you." His voice was barely audible.

She reached out for his hand, but he snatched it back as if her touch had burned him. "But that's what I wanted to talk about…" She took a deep breath. "I'm not leaving. I've decided to stay here on Magnolia Key."

His eyes narrowed. "But what about your daughter? Doesn't she need you now?"

"Let's just say I decided it was time for both my kids to learn to take responsibility for their own lives." She didn't really want to get into all the details with him and how foolish she'd been to actually believe her children needed her. They didn't need *her*, they just needed someone to do the work.

"Oh. I guess Beverly was happy."

She stared at him. That was his reaction? That *Beverly* was pleased?

"I thought maybe we…" She cleared her

throat. "Do you think we could pick up where we left off? We could, uh… see each other again?"

"If you're staying in town, I'm sure we'll see each other. Hard to avoid people on the island."

Was he being deliberately obtuse? "No, I meant… could we… date?" This wasn't working out like she'd planned.

His face hardened, and he clenched his jaw. "I don't think that would be such a good idea. I'm glad you're staying on the island, if that's what makes you happy. But I don't think we should start things up again."

Disappointment surged through her. But could she blame him? She'd called it quits when she decided to move away. He'd been hurt. She saw it in his eyes. Why would he trust her now?

"Are you sure? We could take things slow. See how they work out." She searched his face but saw no sign of him softening his resolve.

"I think it's best if we didn't."

"I guess our joint project on the coastal furniture is scrapped too?"

"I don't think a joint venture like that is a good idea anymore, either. You might change your mind after the baby is born and want to move."

"That's not happening. I'm staying."

He nodded but didn't look like he believed her.

"I'm sorry I hurt you. I didn't mean to. I was just trying to do the right thing, and everything got all messed up."

He just stood there looking at her, not saying a word.

"Okay, well… good night then." She backed away.

"Good night." He closed the door as she stood there.

She slowly turned around and walked back to her cottage, her heart breaking into a million little pieces. She'd had a chance with a really great guy. One she let herself have feelings for. But she ruined her chances.

She walked into her cottage, her footsteps echoing from the wooden boards and ricocheting around the empty room. She walked over and sank onto the couch. The emotions of the day overwhelmed her. From hearing her children talk about her and realizing they would never appreciate her or respect her to this conversation with Dale. And knowing he didn't trust her anymore. Didn't want to date her. Or even work with her. She closed her eyes to hold back her tears.

How was she going to stay in Magnolia and run into him all the time? She lived in his backyard, for Pete's sake. Maybe she'd find another place to move into here on the island. Farther away from Dale. That might help.

But it wouldn't help her broken heart. The heart that had leapt at a chance with Dale. And fluttered when she saw him. A man she could talk to and be herself around. Who didn't try to control her.

An overwhelming sense of loss swept over her, drowning her in the what-ifs. But she couldn't change what happened. She'd just have to take this curve life threw at her and move on. Like she had when Victor left her. She knew how to start over. And she would. She'd make a nice life for herself here in Magnolia.

A life that didn't include Dale.

CHAPTER 26

Maxine and Beverly sat sipping coffee the next afternoon after closing Coastal Coffee. "So you told Dale you were staying?" Beverly asked. "And it made no difference to him?"

"He won't take a chance with me. He doesn't want anything to do with me. I guess I need to find a place to move to here on the island. He certainly doesn't want me living in his backyard."

"You could move into the apartment over the cafe if you want. We'd have to clear it out."

"That's probably a good idea." Though she loved her little cottage and would miss it. She'd made it into a place that felt like home.

"You could try talking to him again."

"It wouldn't do any good. He's made up his mind. I could see it in his eyes. He won't take another chance with me."

"Well, you can't force a person to take a chance, to risk changing their life." Beverly stared at her coffee mug and sat quietly, lost in thought.

Maxine finally broke the silence. "Are you okay? You sound like you're talking about something other than Dale and me."

Beverly looked up, a sad expression on her face. "I am. I'm talking about me. About someone I loved. Someone who wouldn't or couldn't take a chance on me."

"Who? I didn't know you were ever serious about anyone." This surprised her. How had she let them drift apart so far that she didn't even know something like this about Beverly?

"No one knew. We were dating secretly."

"Why?"

"Because his family didn't approve of someone like me. They had big plans for him and I wasn't part of them."

"Who was this guy?" Maxine couldn't believe she'd never known about this.

Beverly sat silently for a moment. "He was... He was Cliff, Eleanor's oldest son."

"No kidding?" She sat back in her chair, stunned. "But he was always…"

"The town troublemaker? Yes, he was. But I came to realize as I got to know him that it was just his way of trying to get his parents' attention. And he craved their approval."

"So, what happened between you two?" She leaned forward. "Why didn't you end up together?"

"I was supposed to meet him at the ferry. We were going to run away together. I was going to give up Coastal Coffee and everything. But I didn't care. I would have done anything to be with Cliff. I… I loved him so much."

"But what happened?"

"I showed up at the ferry landing and he wasn't there. I waited for hours. He never showed up."

"But why?"

"I went back to Coastal Coffee and there was a letter waiting for me. He said his father asked him to go work with his uncle up east and eventually take over that branch of the family business. That he couldn't run off with me because he had to concentrate on this new opportunity. He was going to prove to his father that he could make a success of it."

"But you could have gone with him, couldn't you?"

"He didn't want me… I didn't fit into his plans anymore." Beverly took a sip of her coffee. "But I regret that I never went after him. Talked to him. Told him how I felt about him and how we could make it work. Even if his parents would never approve of me as a match for him."

She sipped her coffee and tried to digest all that Beverly had told her. "You and Cliff. I can't even imagine. My memories of him are just that he was a wild, irresponsible kid."

"He was. But he got this chance to prove himself. And he took it." Beverly shrugged. "So I stayed in Magnolia. Kept Coastal Coffee. Made a life for myself. A good life. But I still harbor disappointment and anger toward Cliff. He just left me waiting there, and then all he left was a letter. Wouldn't even talk to me face to face. I was devastated."

"I'm sorry I wasn't here for you when you were going through all of that."

"Like I wasn't there for you when Victor divorced you?"

"I can't believe we drifted apart so much that we didn't know about major things happening in each other's lives. Let's never let that happen again."

"Good plan." Beverly's lips lifted in a sad smile. "Because I missed having you here to talk to. It's been nice having you back."

"It is nice, isn't it?"

"And since we are so close again, I'm going to give you some advice. Go talk to Dale again. Stand up for what you want. Ask for it. Tell him how you feel about him. Take that risk."

"I think that ship has sailed."

"Give him some time to get used to the idea you're staying here. And on second thought, don't move into the apartment. Stay at the cottage. Let him see you around. Get used to the idea. *Then* talk to him again."

She frowned. "Maybe you're right. That he just needs some time." A tiny sprig of hope started to grow inside her.

Dale was annoyed. Everywhere he turned, there was Maxine. She read books out in the lounge chair in the courtyard. She went out in front of his cottage and sat on the beach, watching the sunsets. She even came by the shop to pick out a small table she wanted to paint for the guest house. *His* guest house. Why had he ever been crazy enough to offer it up to her, anyway?

He half wanted to tell her to find a new place to live. Like on the other side of the island. But another part of him didn't want her to go...

Yes, he did.

He wanted her to find a new place. Didn't he?

How had all of this gotten so complicated?

He looked up at the sound of someone coming into the shop, hoping it wasn't Maxine. Or was he hoping it was?

"Dale, there you are." Miss Eleanor came walking up to him. "I wanted to make sure you're coming to the town council meeting tonight. They're discussing the ridiculous idea of letting that developer come in and put up a high-rise development. I want a good turnout to show how much we oppose the idea."

He'd forgotten the meeting was tonight. And Maxine would probably be there with Beverly. "I'm not sure if I can make it."

"Of course you can." Miss Eleanor pinned him with a hard stare. "You're not saying you're not coming because you're still avoiding Maxine, are you?"

"What? No. Of course not." Not exactly.

"Good, then you'll be there."

"Yes, I'll be there." No one argued with Miss Eleanor.

Eleanor turned and started to walk away, then paused and turned back. "And you know you're being a fool, don't you?"

He raised an eyebrow. "What?"

"About Maxine. It's obvious you care about her. Being afraid of something is no reason to avoid it. That's not how to live your life. And if you let a chance at love pass you by because you're afraid? You might regret it for the rest of your life." She paused and a look of pain crossed her features. "I know I regret it. Every single day of my life," she said softly. Then without another word, she whirled around and slipped out the door.

Miss Eleanor had given up on someone she loved? He'd never heard anything about a romance before she married Mr. Griffin. Not a word. But the pain on her face was impossible to ignore. Someone had hurt her deeply. Or maybe she'd hurt herself with the choice she'd made.

Who ever thought he'd be taking advice

from Miss Eleanor? But maybe she was right. Should he face his fear and try again with Maxine? But what if she changed her mind after the baby was born? Or just got tired of island life? What if things didn't work out with them if they tried again?

But if he didn't try, would he live to have regrets, just like Miss Eleanor?

He scrubbed his hand over his face. Things just seemed to get more complicated at every turn.

CHAPTER 27

Maxine and Beverly sat next to Miss Eleanor at the council meeting that night. Miss Eleanor must have made her rounds because half the town residents were crammed into the chairs and standing along the walls, waiting for the meeting to begin. No one in town went against Miss Eleanor's wishes.

Maxine spied Dale as he came in but wasn't surprised when he took a place against the wall on the far side of the room. About as far away from her as he could get.

The room quieted down as the council members came in and took their seats at the table in front. The mayor called the meeting to order.

"I know you all want your say about any changes we might propose to the island's building regulations. But we need to consider what's best for the town. Things will change with the bridge. We'll have more people coming to town. We'll need places for them to stay. We're about to hit a boom time for Magnolia. One that's long overdue."

"The man's a fool," Eleanor whispered loudly. Two men sitting behind them chuckled.

"And to start the meeting, I'd like to introduce you to the man who bought the property and let him explain his plans. I believe they are well thought out plans and will benefit everyone."

A man walked in from the side of the room and Eleanor gasped. Then Beverly gasped. Maxine stared at the man. He looked vaguely familiar.

"I'd like to introduce…" The mayor swung out his arm. "Cliff Griffin. Some of you may remember him from when he grew up here."

Maxine swung her gaze from Eleanor to Beverly. Beverly's face had drained of color, while Eleanor's was a fiery red.

"Glad to be here to have a chance to talk to

y'all," Cliff said. "I think you'll see these plans are very doable for the town. It's time we moved on and brought our little town up to date, don't you think?"

The room burst into a rumble of conversation.

Beverly reached over and took her hand, squeezing it, but her eyes never left Cliff. Maxine covered her hand and squeezed back in support.

Miss Eleanor stood up and the room went silent. "I think our little town is just fine like it is. Not that you'd know that since you haven't been back in years."

"Evening, Mama. I see you're disagreeing with what I'm doing as usual." He gave her a boyish smile.

Everyone started talking again, and the mayor banged his gavel to no avail. He finally stood up and shouted. "Quiet, or I'll throw you all out."

As people settled back down, the mayor stepped aside. "Now, Cliff, how about you continue?"

"Mama, that okay with you?" Cliff winked. Miss Eleanor glowered. He gave a five-minute presentation while Eleanor scowled the whole time. "So we're asking for a variance on how many units per building and the height. We'd need to go at least six stories for this to be a profitable venture."

Eleanor rose again. "And why are your profits any of our concern?"

"Well, they're family profits, Mama. You know I took over our uncle's business. Our family would profit. And the whole town, too, of course, from the hospitality taxes the people would pay and bringing in more customers for every business in town."

"You're going to ruin the town with a project like this. The reason we like our town is it is quaint and quiet and... well, you wouldn't understand. You never appreciated it." Eleanor sat down.

Resident after resident stood to speak. Maxine was surprised that a good portion of them supported the variance and embraced the change. Though the vast majority were still opposed to it.

"We're going to table this for tonight," the mayor said. "We'll give you time to write to the council with any concerns you have. We'll take this up again at next month's meeting. But now we're adjourned."

Cliff walked over to where they were standing. "Mama, Beverly." He nodded at them, then looked at her for a moment, recognition dawning in his eyes. "And Maxine, right?"

"Right." How could he stand there looking all innocent? She knew what he did all those years ago to Beverly, and now he was trying to ruin their town.

Miss Eleanor glared at Cliff. "You could have let me know you were coming. That you were behind all this nonsense."

"It's good to see you, too, Mama."

"I'll have to make up the guest room when we get home since you didn't give me the courtesy of knowing in advance you were visiting."

"Only one night, Mama. And I have a room at Darlene's B&B. Didn't want to put you out any. And I have to meet with a few people in town before I leave."

Beverly stood silently at her side, saying not a word, but her gaze was locked on Cliff.

"Well, ladies, I should take my leave. Good seeing you all." He nodded once, took a long look at Beverly, then walked away.

Eleanor watched him leave, then turned to them. "I had no idea he was behind all this. I'll do anything I can to stop him." A determined look settled on her features, then she turned around and left.

Maxine squeezed Beverly's hand again. "Are you okay?"

"I honestly don't know. This was the last thing in the world I expected tonight. I can't believe Cliff is behind all this. I thought he loved the island as much as we do. He knows this will change everything."

"I wasn't really asking about the variance. I was asking how you are with seeing Cliff again."

"To be honest? I'm surprised how much it still hurts to see him after all these years. And it appears he hasn't changed. He's still doing exactly what he wants, no matter who it hurts." Beverly turned and walked out of the room.

She hurried after her. "Here, let me walk home with you."

"You don't have to do that."

"I want to. I want to make sure you're okay."

Beverly paused under the lamppost. "I'm okay. I promise. Or I will be. I just need some time to adjust to seeing him again. You go on home. I'll be fine. I need some time alone."

"Okay, if you're sure." Maxine frowned as Beverly headed down the sidewalk. Beverly had a lot to think about tonight. To process. But then, she herself had a lot to think about. Like trying to talk to Dale again.

CHAPTER 28

Beverly walked slowly back to her cottage trying to process the fact that she'd seen Cliff again. After all these years. He was still devilishly handsome, and it irked her that she'd noticed it.

She'd spent so many years pushing him out of her mind, giving her heart time to heal. And now with one look at him, her heart exploded with the same exact pain she'd felt all those years ago.

She turned at the sound of someone walking up behind her.

Cliff.

"Hey."

Hey? That's all he had to say? Hey?

"I… uh… I guess I should have let you know I was coming to town." He shifted from foot to foot. "But I didn't want people to know I was behind this development until I had a chance to show my presentation. Get more people to support it."

"Always doing what's best for you, aren't you?" The words just slipped out as anger tromped through her.

"No, I just… I need this to work out. This development, I mean. Not that Dad is around anymore to see my success… or failure."

She ignored the flash of pain in his eyes. The same longing she used to see when he was desperately trying to please his father.

"I hope it doesn't work out. That you leave. And leave our island alone. Of all the places in the world, why did you choose this one to develop?"

"Because… it was a good opportunity with the bridge being built."

"And you don't care that it will ruin the atmosphere of the island? Once one high-rise gets approved, it will pave the way for others."

"It's time Magnolia moved into this century, don't you think?"

She clenched her jaw. "I'm fairly certain you don't care what I think or what I need. You've proven that."

"Don't be like that. We were just kids back then. And I had a chance to show my dad what I could do. I couldn't pass it up."

"But you could leave me behind. Standing at the ferry. Alone. For hours."

He gave her a sheepish look. "Yeah, that was wrong. But I left you a letter."

"Because you were too chicken to talk to me face to face. I deserved better."

He sighed. "You did. I was young then. I handled it poorly."

Poorly? How about heartlessly?

"I was kind of hoping to get your support. If you support this development, I know a lot of other townspeople will follow your lead."

"I'll tell you one thing, Cliff Griffin." She poked her finger at his chest. "I'll fight you with everything I have to make sure this development never happens. Never."

She whirled around and hurried off, leaving him behind her. Leaving her memories of what they'd once had behind her. The only thing in front of her was her immense desire that he didn't get his way. She'd make sure to ruin all his plans for his stupid development. Every last little plan. Then maybe, maybe, she'd feel like they were even. And she'd put him behind her once and for all.

CHAPTER 29

Maxine went out early the next morning with her coffee. She was working the later shift today so had lots of time. Though she did want to get to Coastal Coffee and see how Beverly was doing. It must have been a shock to see Cliff after all these years. And painful. Why were relationships always so hard? And complicated?

"Maxine?"

She looked up, surprised to see Dale standing beside her.

"Mind if I join you?"

That surprised her even more. "No, please. Sit."

He dropped down beside her. "I thought maybe we could talk."

"I thought you said we didn't have anything to talk about." She eyed him carefully, trying to judge his mood.

"I was being stubborn. And a fool, according to Miss Eleanor."

"Miss Eleanor called you a fool?"

"She did." He nodded sheepishly. "And I don't think she was that far from the truth. She also said that some things are worth the risk. That if we don't take chances, we may live with regrets for the rest of our lives."

That tiny piece of hope inside her grew a bit larger.

He took her hand. "And I don't want to have regrets for the rest of my life. I don't. I'm not saying I'm not worried that you'll change your mind and leave. I am worried. But... I'm willing to risk that for a chance to see where all this is headed. You and me."

"You want to try again?" She wanted to make sure she heard him correctly.

"I do. Will you go out with me again? On a date. And another one after that." He brushed her hair back from her face, trailing his finger along her cheek. "And I think we should reconsider our joint effort on a coastal decor corner of my shop. That is, if you still want to."

"Oh, I want to."

"You want to do the coastal decor or you want to date me?" He cocked his head to the side.

"Yes." She grinned. "Both."

Beverly's voice played in her head. Tell him what you want. What you need. Stand up for yourself.

She jumped up from the sand. "And one more thing."

"What's that?" He looked at her closely.

"I'd really like to have that first kiss."

He grinned and jumped up to stand beside her. Her heart did a triple beat.

He leaned in close and finally, finally kissed her. Gently at first, then he deepened the kiss, taking her breath away. When he finally stepped back, she struggled to gather her wits about her.

His grin still tugged at the corners of his mouth. "Pretty nice kiss, but I think we should keep practicing until we get it perfect."

She nodded, unable to find her words. And he kissed her again. Then they settled back on the sand as the sky lit up with pink and yellow as the new day began, starting afresh. Just like their relationship sprawled out before them, just waiting to see what they made of it.

I hope you enjoyed the start of the Magnolia Key series. We'll find out more about Beverly and Cliff as the series continues. Try book two, Encore Echoes. A mysterious woman comes to town and buys the Magnolia Key theater and restores it to its former glory. And there will be a few more hints about the town's mysterious past...

As always, thank you so much for reading my books. I truly appreciate all of you. I hope the books bring you a bit of escape and joy.

Until next time,

Kay

ALSO BY KAY CORRELL

COMFORT CROSSING ~ THE SERIES

The Shop on Main - Book One

The Memory Box - Book Two

The Christmas Cottage - A Holiday Novella
(Book 2.5)

The Letter - Book Three

The Christmas Scarf - A Holiday Novella (Book 3.5)

The Magnolia Cafe - Book Four

The Unexpected Wedding - Book Five

The Wedding in the Grove (crossover short story
between series - Josephine and Paul from The Letter.)

LIGHTHOUSE POINT ~ THE SERIES

Wish Upon a Shell - Book One

Wedding on the Beach - Book Two

Love at the Lighthouse - Book Three

Cottage near the Point - Book Four

Return to the Island - Book Five

Bungalow by the Bay - Book Six

Christmas Comes to Lighthouse Point - Book Seven

CHARMING INN ~ Return to Lighthouse Point

One Simple Wish - Book One

Two of a Kind - Book Two

Three Little Things - Book Three

Four Short Weeks - Book Four

Five Years or So - Book Five

Six Hours Away - Book Six

Charming Christmas - Book Seven

SWEET RIVER ~ THE SERIES

A Dream to Believe in - Book One

A Memory to Cherish - Book Two

A Song to Remember - Book Three

A Time to Forgive - Book Four

A Summer of Secrets - Book Five

A Moment in the Moonlight - Book Six

MOONBEAM BAY ~ THE SERIES

The Parker Women - Book One

The Parker Cafe - Book Two

A Heather Parker Original - Book Three

The Parker Family Secret - Book Four

Grace Parker's Peach Pie - Book Five

The Perks of Being a Parker - Book Six

BLUE HERON COTTAGES ~ THE SERIES

Memories of the Beach - Book One

Walks along the Shore - Book Two

Bookshop near the Coast - Book Three

Restaurant on the Wharf - Book Four

Lilacs by the Sea - Book Five

Flower Shop on Magnolia - Book Six

Christmas by the Bay - Book Seven

Sea Glass from the Past - Book Eight

MAGNOLIA KEY ~ THE SERIES

Saltwater Sunrise - Book One

Encore Echoes - Book Two

And more to come

WIND CHIME BEACH ~ A stand-alone novel

INDIGO BAY ~

Sweet Days by the Bay - Kay's complete collection of stories in the Indigo Bay series

ABOUT THE AUTHOR

Kay Correll is a USA Today bestselling author of sweet, heartwarming stories that are a cross between women's fiction and contemporary romance. She is known for her charming small towns, quirky townsfolk, and the enduring strong friendships between the women in her books.

Kay splits her time between the southwest coast of Florida and the Midwest of the U.S. and can often be found out and about with her camera, taking a myriad of photographs, often incorporating them into her book covers. When not lost in her writing or photography, she can be found spending time with her ever-supportive husband, knitting, or playing with her puppies - a cavalier who is too cute for his own good and a naughty but adorable Australian shepherd. Their five boys are all grown now and while she misses the rowdy boy-noise chaos, she is thoroughly enjoying her empty nest years.

Learn more about Kay and her books at kaycorrell.com

While you're there, sign up for her newsletter to hear about new releases, sales, and giveaways.

WHERE TO FIND ME:
My shop: shop.kaycorrell.com
My author website: kaycorrell.com
authorcontact@kaycorrell.com

Join my Facebook Reader Group. We have lots of fun and you'll hear about sales and new releases first!
www.facebook.com/groups/KayCorrell/

I love to hear from my readers. Feel free to contact me at authorcontact@kaycorrell.com

facebook.com/KayCorrellAuthor
instagram.com/kaycorrell
pinterest.com/kaycorrellauthor
amazon.com/author/kaycorrell
bookbub.com/authors/kay-correll